Wait Till
Helen Comes

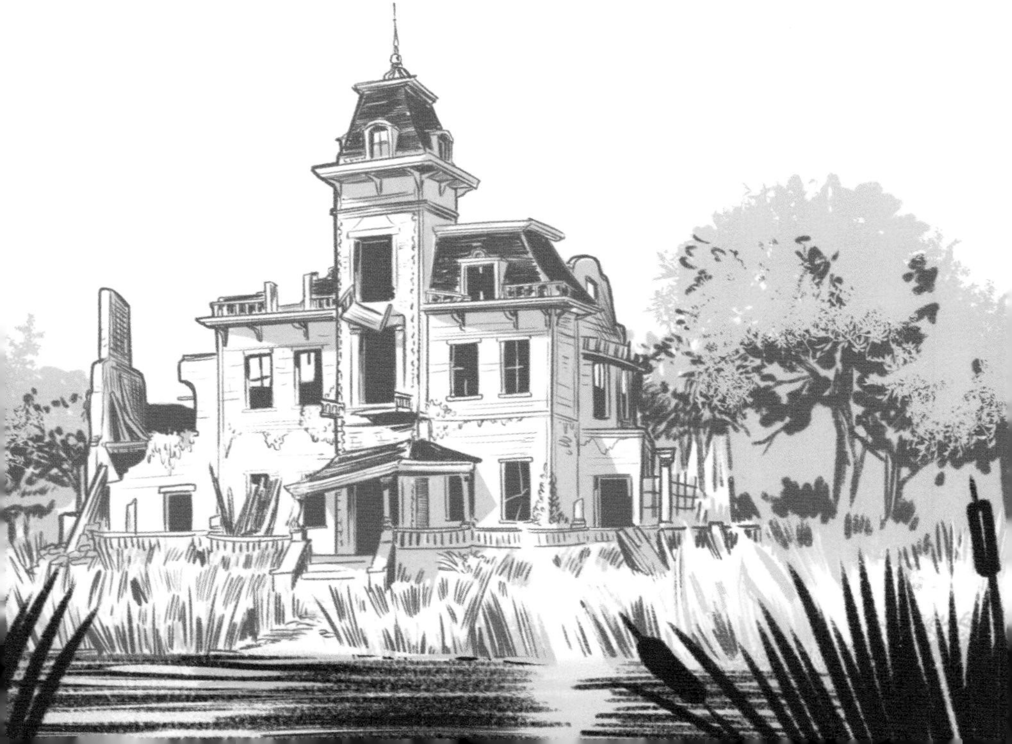

MARY DOWNING HAHN

Wait Till Helen Comes

a ghost story graphic novel

Adapted by Scott Peterson, Meredith Laxton,
and Russ Badgett

Clarion Books
Imprints of HarperCollins*Publishers*

HARPER alley

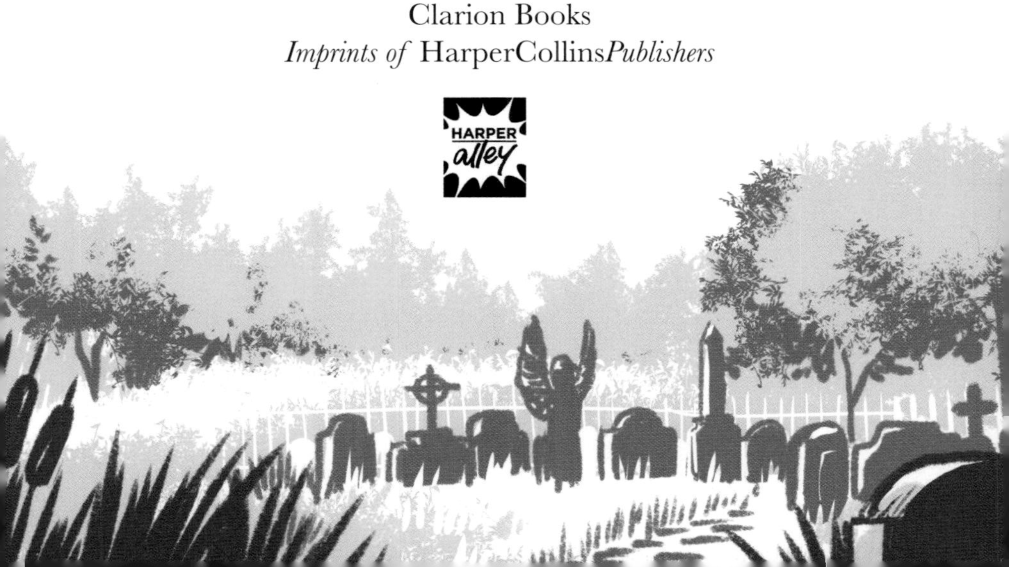

For my kids for being understanding as to why dinner is always late.
And for Meredith for doing such an amazing job on the art.
And, as always, here's to Story.
—S.P.

To my mom, who gives me the courage to face my fears everyday.
Thank you for everything.
—M.L.

Clarion Books is an imprint of HarperCollins Publishers.
HarperAlley is an imprint of HarperCollins Publishers.

Wait Till Helen Comes Graphic Novel
Copyright © 2022 by HarperCollins Publishers LLC
Adapted from *Wait Till Helen Comes* by Mary Downing Hahn
Copyright © 1986 by Mary Downing Hahn
Text copyright © 2022 by Scott Peterson
Illustrations copyright © 2022 by Meredith Laxton

ISBN 978-0-35-853690-1—ISBN 978-0-35-853689-5 (pbk.)

The artist used Clip Studio to create the digital illustrations for this book.
Typography by Bones Leopard and Pete Friedrich

22 23 24 25 26 EP 10 9 8 7 6 5 4 3 2 1

First Edition

Wait Till Helen Comes

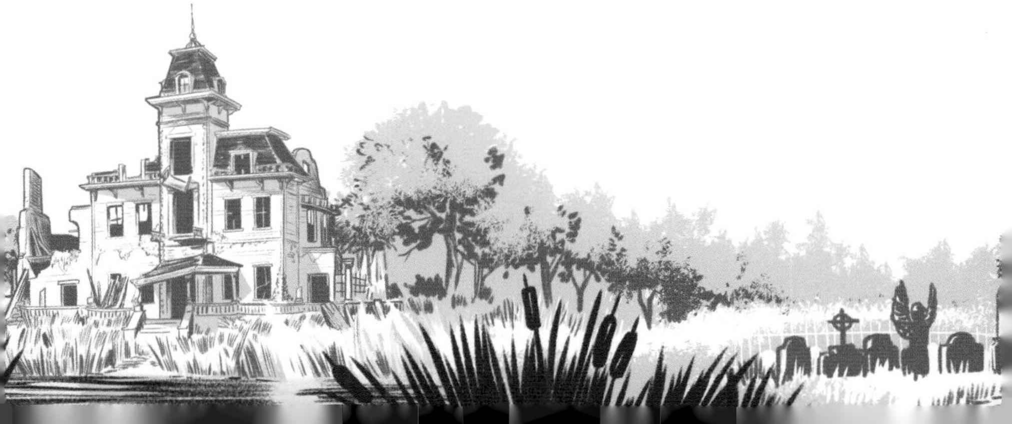

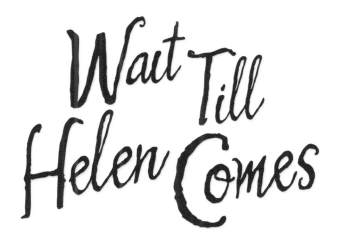

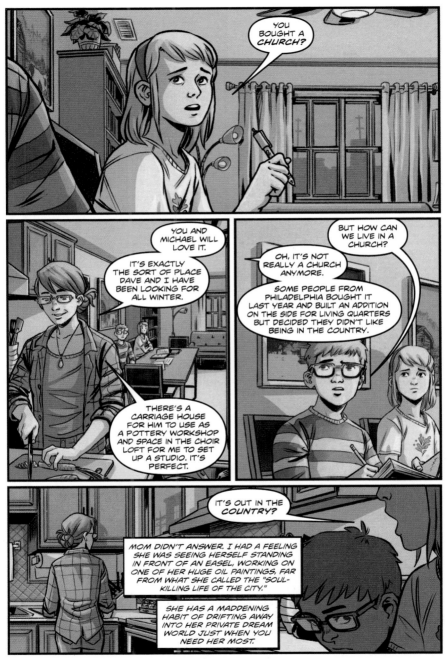

YOU BOUGHT A *CHURCH*?

YOU AND MICHAEL WILL LOVE IT.

IT'S EXACTLY THE SORT OF PLACE DAVE AND I HAVE BEEN LOOKING FOR ALL WINTER.

THERE'S A CARRIAGE HOUSE FOR HIM TO USE AS A POTTERY WORKSHOP AND SPACE IN THE CHOIR LOFT FOR ME TO SET UP A STUDIO. IT'S PERFECT.

BUT HOW CAN WE LIVE IN A CHURCH?

OH, IT'S NOT REALLY A CHURCH ANYMORE.

SOME PEOPLE FROM PHILADELPHIA BOUGHT IT LAST YEAR AND BUILT AN ADDITION ON THE SIDE FOR LIVING QUARTERS BUT DECIDED THEY DIDN'T LIKE BEING IN THE COUNTRY.

IT'S OUT IN THE *COUNTRY*?

MOM DIDN'T ANSWER. I HAD A FEELING SHE WAS SEEING HERSELF STANDING IN FRONT OF AN EASEL, WORKING ON ONE OF HER HUGE OIL PAINTINGS, FAR FROM WHAT SHE CALLED THE "SOUL-KILLING LIFE OF THE CITY."

SHE HAS A MADDENING HABIT OF DRIFTING AWAY INTO HER PRIVATE DREAM WORLD JUST WHEN YOU NEED HER MOST.

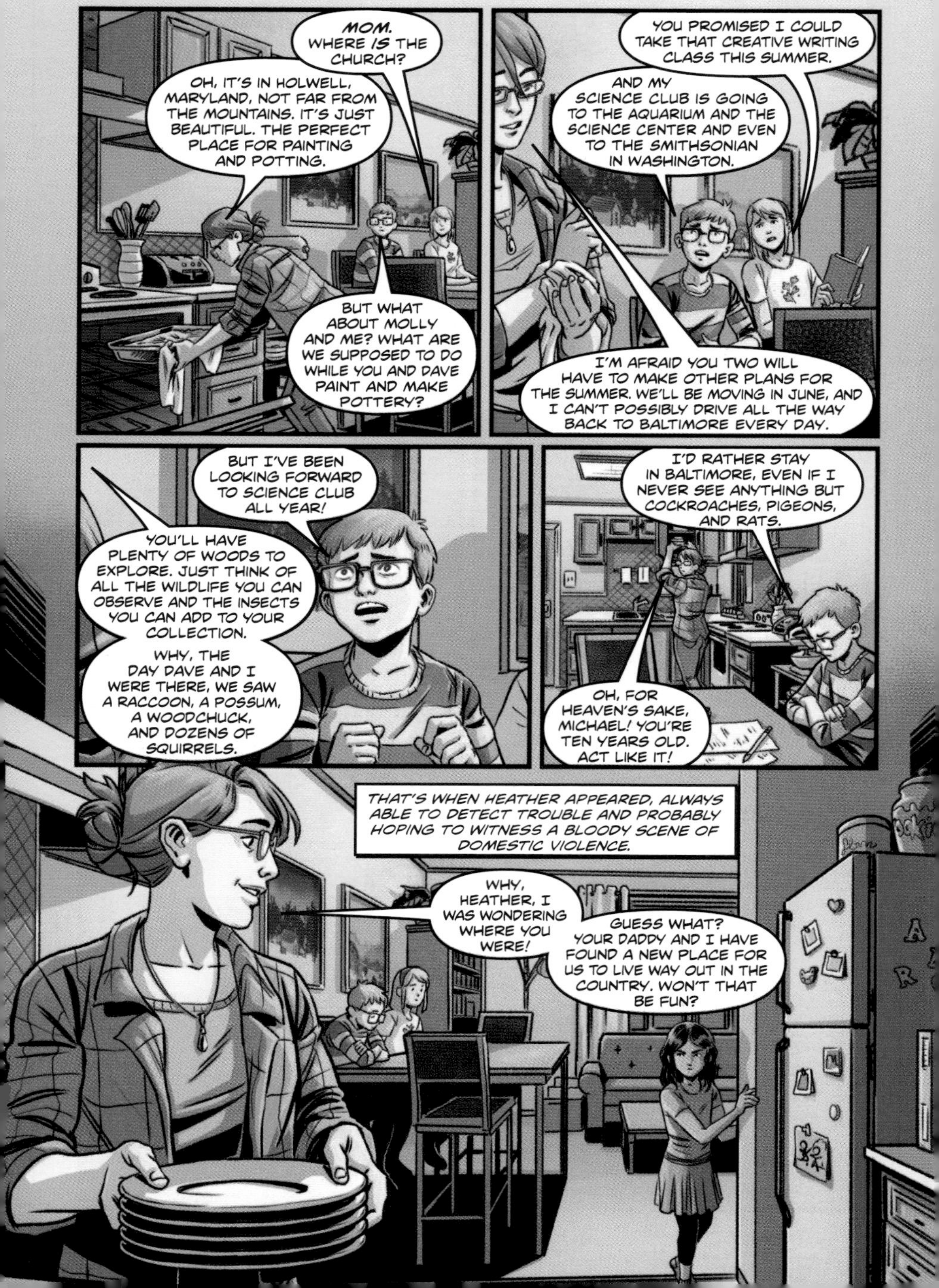
MOM. WHERE IS THE CHURCH?
OH, IT'S IN HOLWELL, MARYLAND, NOT FAR FROM THE MOUNTAINS. IT'S JUST BEAUTIFUL. THE PERFECT PLACE FOR PAINTING AND POTTING.
BUT WHAT ABOUT MOLLY AND ME? WHAT ARE WE SUPPOSED TO DO WHILE YOU AND DAVE PAINT AND MAKE POTTERY?
YOU PROMISED I COULD TAKE THAT CREATIVE WRITING CLASS THIS SUMMER.
AND MY SCIENCE CLUB IS GOING TO THE AQUARIUM AND THE SCIENCE CENTER AND EVEN TO THE SMITHSONIAN IN WASHINGTON.
I'M AFRAID YOU TWO WILL HAVE TO MAKE OTHER PLANS FOR THE SUMMER. WE'LL BE MOVING IN JUNE, AND I CAN'T POSSIBLY DRIVE ALL THE WAY BACK TO BALTIMORE EVERY DAY.
BUT I'VE BEEN LOOKING FORWARD TO SCIENCE CLUB ALL YEAR!
YOU'LL HAVE PLENTY OF WOODS TO EXPLORE. JUST THINK OF ALL THE WILDLIFE YOU CAN OBSERVE AND THE INSECTS YOU CAN ADD TO YOUR COLLECTION.
WHY, THE DAY DAVE AND I WERE THERE, WE SAW A RACCOON, A POSSUM, A WOODCHUCK, AND DOZENS OF SQUIRRELS.
I'D RATHER STAY IN BALTIMORE, EVEN IF I NEVER SEE ANYTHING BUT COCKROACHES, PIGEONS, AND RATS.
OH, FOR HEAVEN'S SAKE, MICHAEL! YOU'RE TEN YEARS OLD. ACT LIKE IT!
THAT'S WHEN HEATHER APPEARED, ALWAYS ABLE TO DETECT TROUBLE AND PROBABLY HOPING TO WITNESS A BLOODY SCENE OF DOMESTIC VIOLENCE.
WHY, HEATHER, I WAS WONDERING WHERE YOU WERE!
GUESS WHAT? YOUR DADDY AND I HAVE FOUND A NEW PLACE FOR US TO LIVE WAY OUT IN THE COUNTRY. WON'T THAT BE FUN?

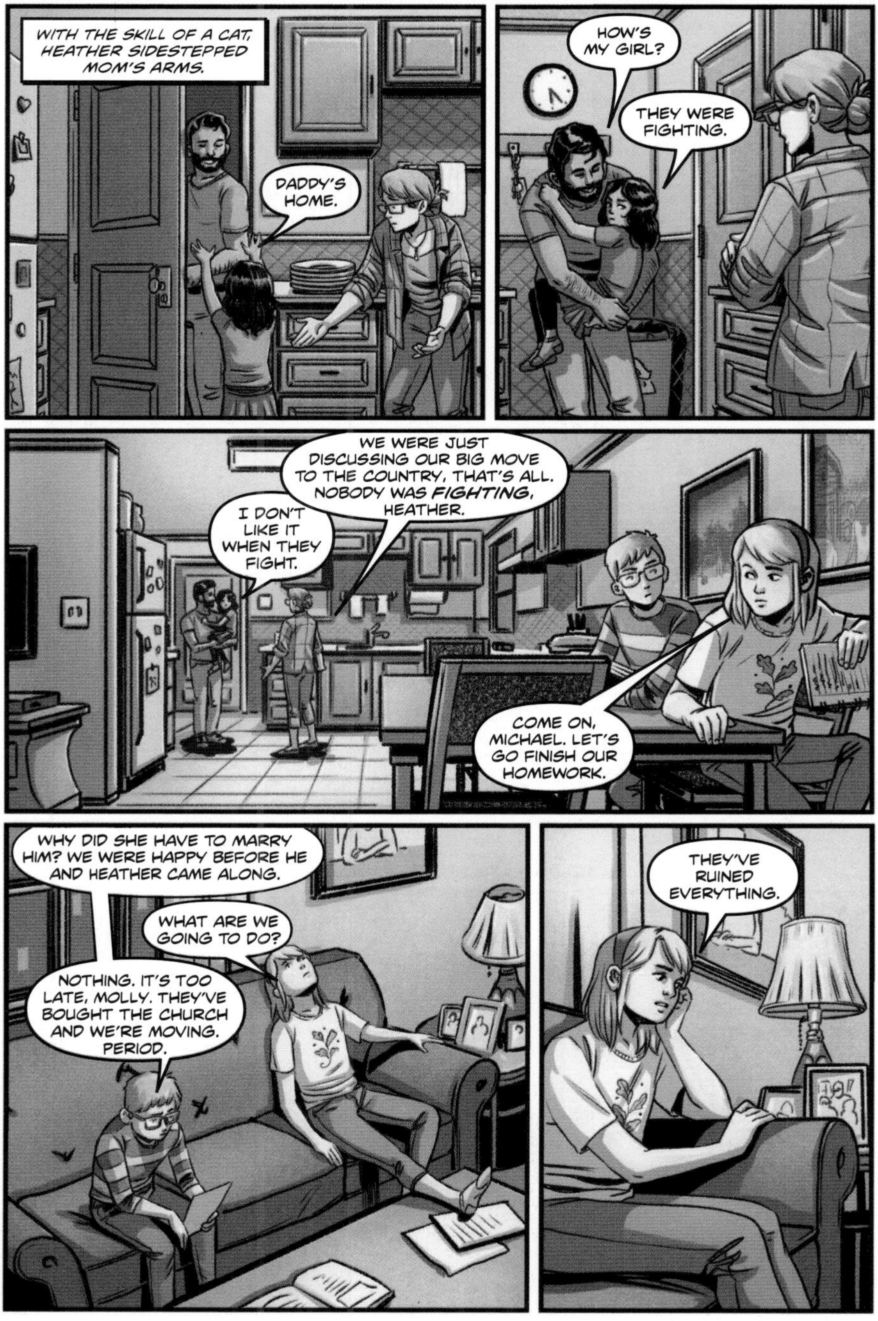
WITH THE SKILL OF A CAT, HEATHER SIDESTEPPED MOM'S ARMS.
DADDY'S HOME.
HOW'S MY GIRL?
THEY WERE FIGHTING.
I DON'T LIKE IT WHEN THEY FIGHT.
WE WERE JUST DISCUSSING OUR BIG MOVE TO THE COUNTRY, THAT'S ALL. NOBODY WAS *FIGHTING*, HEATHER.
COME ON, MICHAEL. LET'S GO FINISH OUR HOMEWORK.
WHY DID SHE HAVE TO MARRY HIM? WE WERE HAPPY BEFORE HE AND HEATHER CAME ALONG.
WHAT ARE WE GOING TO DO?
NOTHING. IT'S TOO LATE, MOLLY. THEY'VE BOUGHT THE CHURCH AND WE'RE MOVING. PERIOD.
THEY'VE RUINED EVERYTHING.

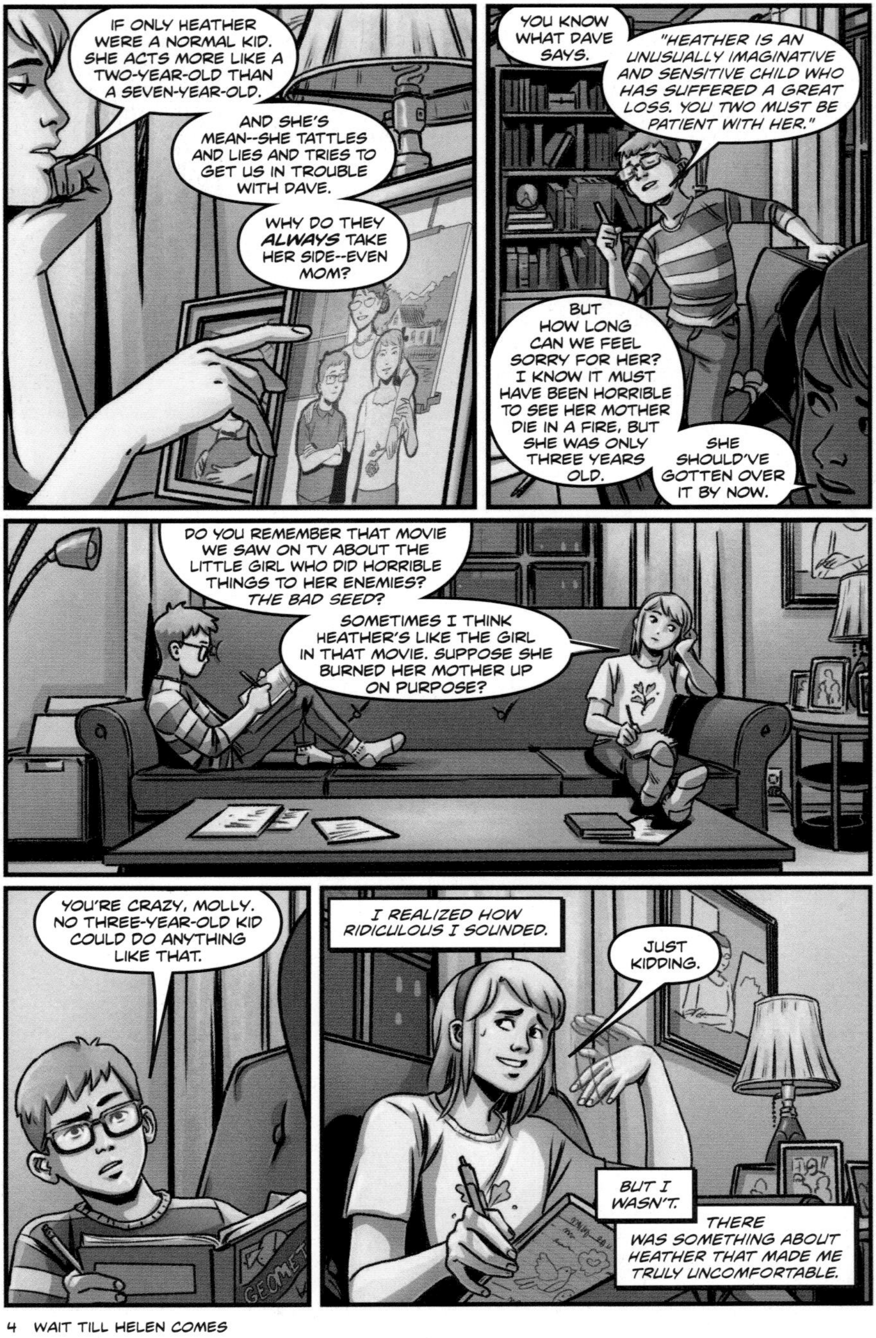
IF ONLY HEATHER WERE A NORMAL KID. SHE ACTS MORE LIKE A TWO-YEAR-OLD THAN A SEVEN-YEAR-OLD.
AND SHE'S MEAN--SHE TATTLES AND LIES AND TRIES TO GET US IN TROUBLE WITH DAVE.
WHY DO THEY ***ALWAYS*** TAKE HER SIDE--EVEN MOM?
YOU KNOW WHAT DAVE SAYS.
"HEATHER IS AN UNUSUALLY IMAGINATIVE AND SENSITIVE CHILD WHO HAS SUFFERED A GREAT LOSS. YOU TWO MUST BE PATIENT WITH HER."
BUT HOW LONG CAN WE FEEL SORRY FOR HER? I KNOW IT MUST HAVE BEEN HORRIBLE TO SEE HER MOTHER DIE IN A FIRE, BUT SHE WAS ONLY THREE YEARS OLD.
SHE SHOULD'VE GOTTEN OVER IT BY NOW.
DO YOU REMEMBER THAT MOVIE WE SAW ON TV ABOUT THE LITTLE GIRL WHO DID HORRIBLE THINGS TO HER ENEMIES? *THE BAD SEED?*
SOMETIMES I THINK HEATHER'S LIKE THE GIRL IN THAT MOVIE. SUPPOSE SHE BURNED HER MOTHER UP ON PURPOSE?
YOU'RE CRAZY, MOLLY. NO THREE-YEAR-OLD KID COULD DO ANYTHING LIKE THAT.
I REALIZED HOW RIDICULOUS I SOUNDED.
JUST KIDDING.
BUT I WASN'T.
THERE WAS SOMETHING ABOUT HEATHER THAT MADE ME TRULY UNCOMFORTABLE.

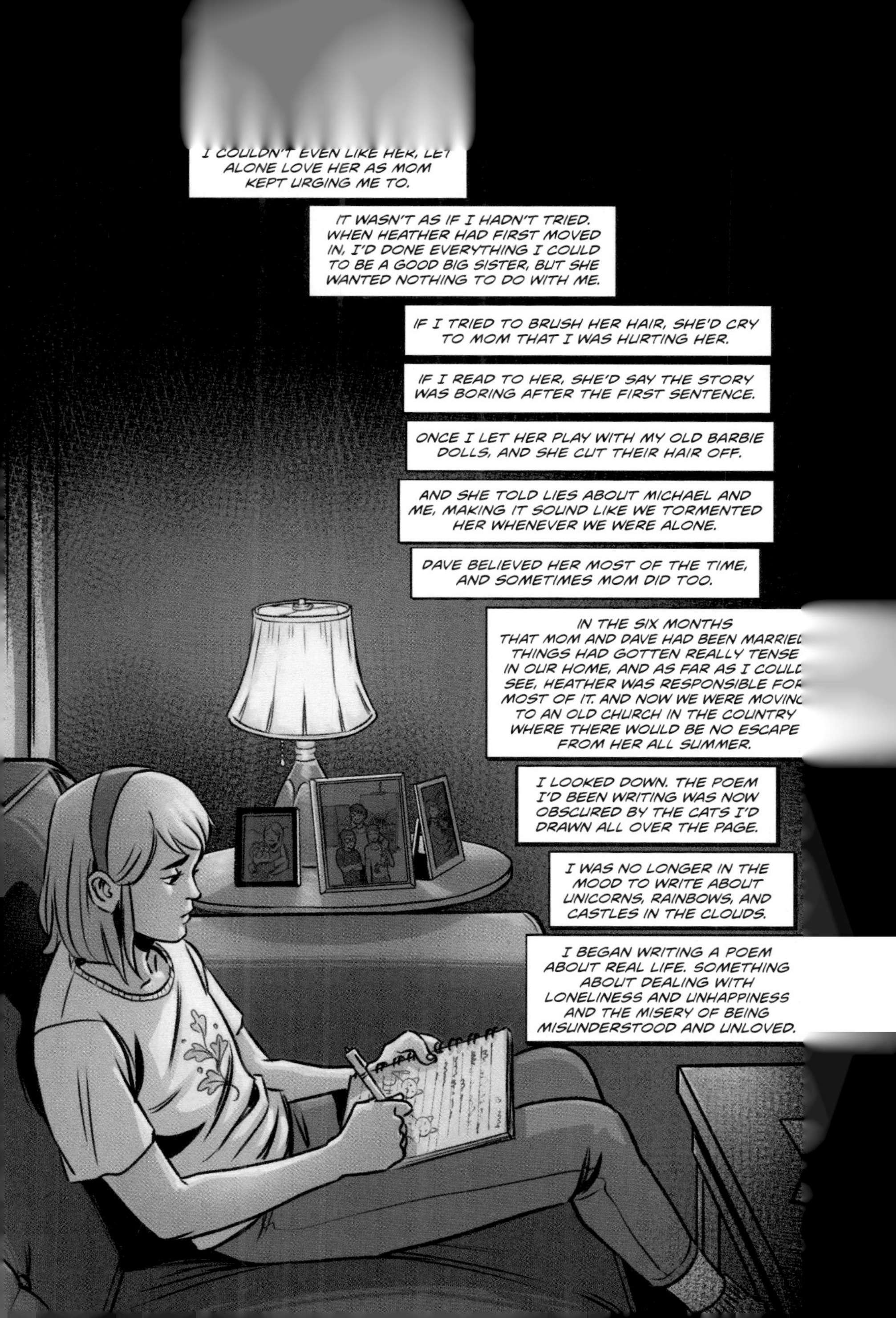
I COULDN'T EVEN LIKE HER, LET ALONE LOVE HER AS MOM KEPT URGING ME TO.
IT WASN'T AS IF I HADN'T TRIED. WHEN HEATHER HAD FIRST MOVED IN, I'D DONE EVERYTHING I COULD TO BE A GOOD BIG SISTER, BUT SHE WANTED NOTHING TO DO WITH ME.
IF I TRIED TO BRUSH HER HAIR, SHE'D CRY TO MOM THAT I WAS HURTING HER.
IF I READ TO HER, SHE'D SAY THE STORY WAS BORING AFTER THE FIRST SENTENCE.
ONCE I LET HER PLAY WITH MY OLD BARBIE DOLLS, AND SHE CUT THEIR HAIR OFF.
AND SHE TOLD LIES ABOUT MICHAEL AND ME, MAKING IT SOUND LIKE WE TORMENTED HER WHENEVER WE WERE ALONE.
DAVE BELIEVED HER MOST OF THE TIME, AND SOMETIMES MOM DID TOO.
IN THE SIX MONTHS THAT MOM AND DAVE HAD BEEN MARRIE THINGS HAD GOTTEN REALLY TENSE IN OUR HOME, AND AS FAR AS I COUL SEE, HEATHER WAS RESPONSIBLE FO MOST OF IT. AND NOW WE WERE MOVIN TO AN OLD CHURCH IN THE COUNTRY WHERE THERE WOULD BE NO ESCAPE FROM HER ALL SUMMER.
I LOOKED DOWN. THE POEM I'D BEEN WRITING WAS NOW OBSCURED BY THE CATS I'D DRAWN ALL OVER THE PAGE.
I WAS NO LONGER IN THE MOOD TO WRITE ABOUT UNICORNS, RAINBOWS, AND CASTLES IN THE CLOUDS.
I BEGAN WRITING A POEM ABOUT REAL LIFE. SOMETHING ABOUT DEALING WITH LONELINESS AND UNHAPPINESS AND THE MISERY OF BEING MISUNDERSTOOD AND UNLOVED.

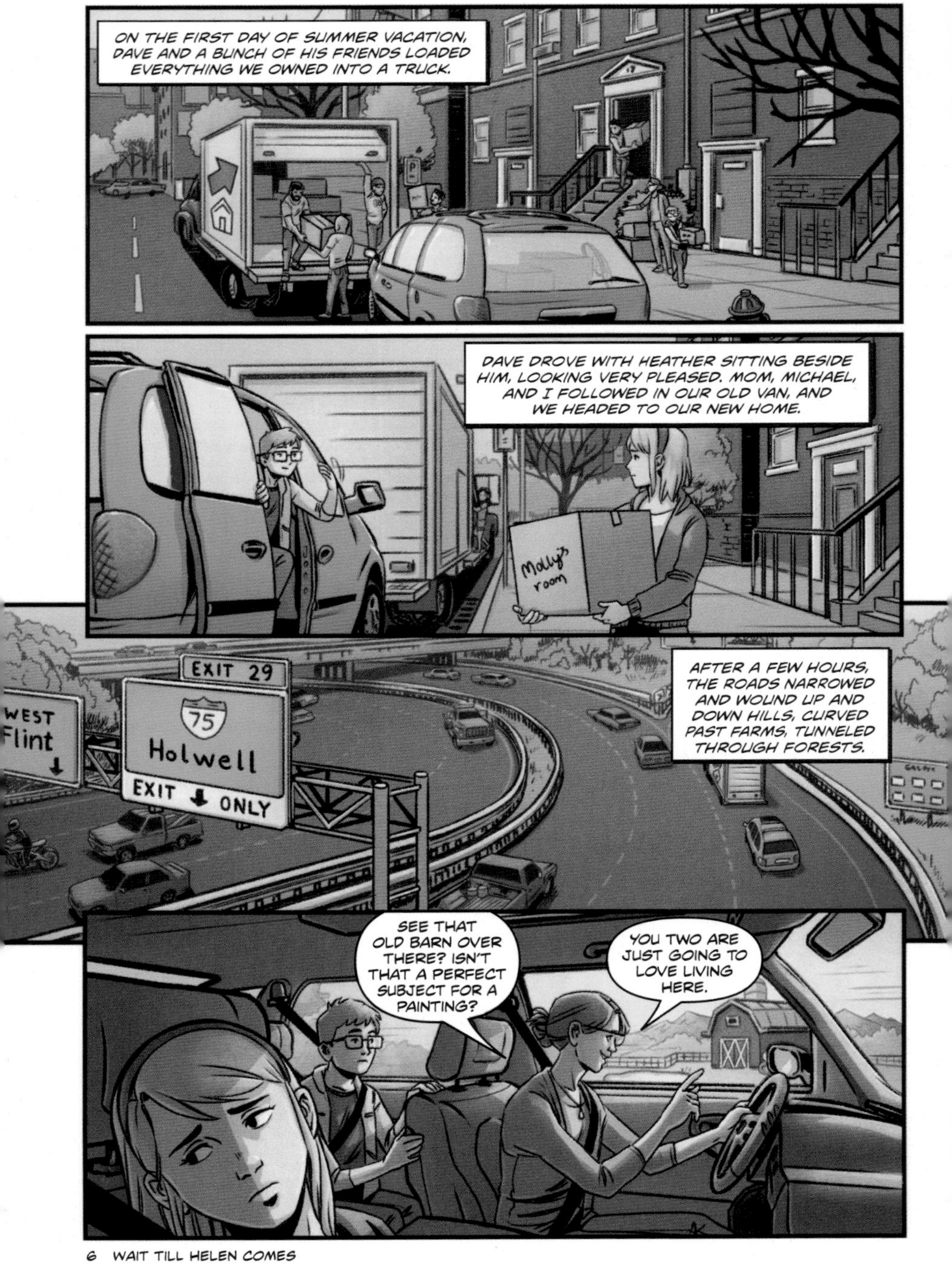
ON THE FIRST DAY OF SUMMER VACATION, DAVE AND A BUNCH OF HIS FRIENDS LOADED EVERYTHING WE OWNED INTO A TRUCK.
DAVE DROVE WITH HEATHER SITTING BESIDE HIM, LOOKING VERY PLEASED. MOM, MICHAEL, AND I FOLLOWED IN OUR OLD VAN, AND WE HEADED TO OUR NEW HOME.
Molly's room
EXIT 29
75
Holwell
EXIT ONLY
WEST
Flint
AFTER A FEW HOURS, THE ROADS NARROWED AND WOUND UP AND DOWN HILLS, CURVED PAST FARMS, TUNNELED THROUGH FORESTS.
SEE THAT OLD BARN OVER THERE? ISN'T THAT A PERFECT SUBJECT FOR A PAINTING?
YOU TWO ARE JUST GOING TO LOVE LIVING HERE.

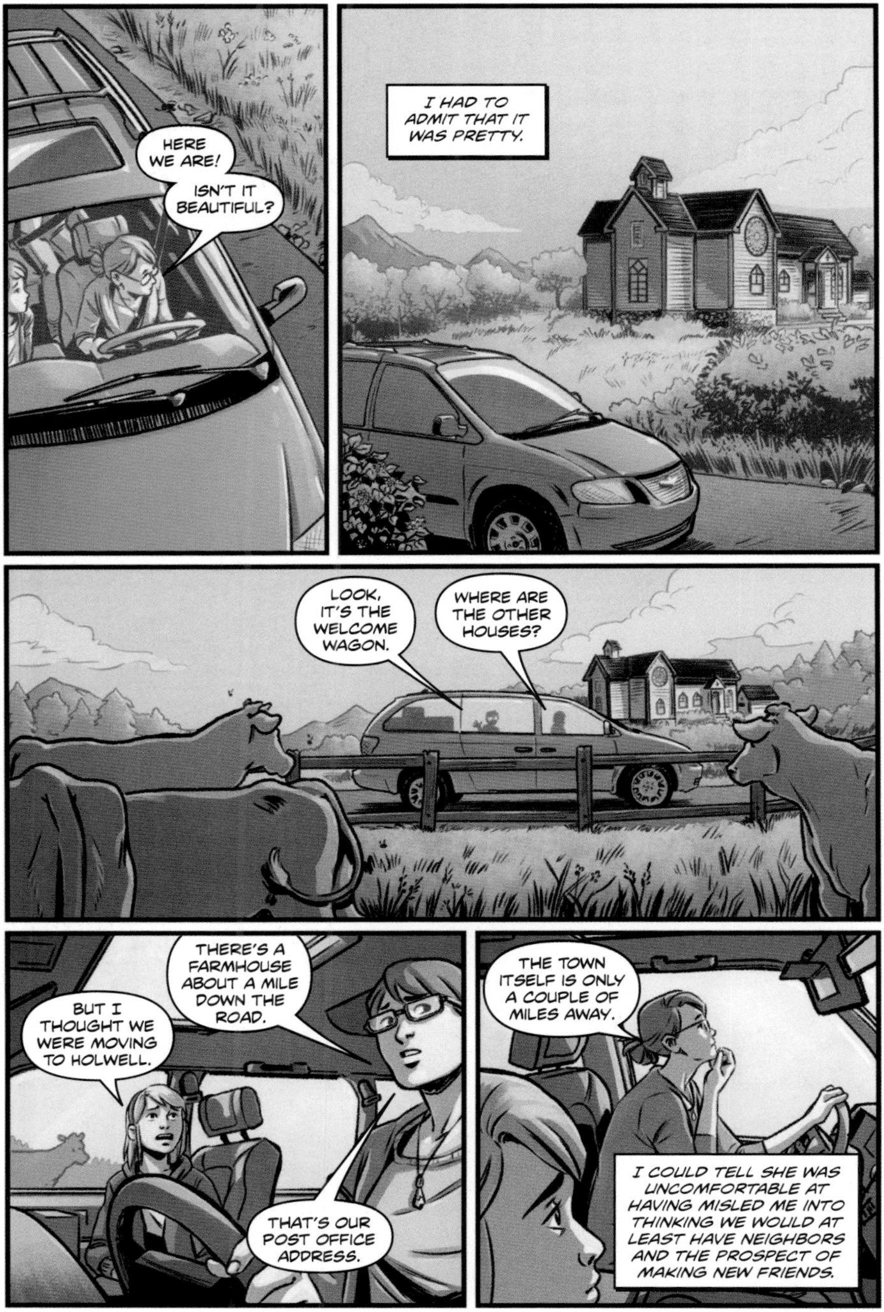
HERE WE ARE!
ISN'T IT BEAUTIFUL?
I HAD TO ADMIT THAT IT WAS PRETTY.
LOOK, IT'S THE WELCOME WAGON.
WHERE ARE THE OTHER HOUSES?
THERE'S A FARMHOUSE ABOUT A MILE DOWN THE ROAD.
BUT I THOUGHT WE WERE MOVING TO HOLWELL.
THAT'S OUR POST OFFICE ADDRESS.
THE TOWN ITSELF IS ONLY A COUPLE OF MILES AWAY.
I COULD TELL SHE WAS UNCOMFORTABLE AT HAVING MISLED ME INTO THINKING WE WOULD AT LEAST HAVE NEIGHBORS AND THE PROSPECT OF MAKING NEW FRIENDS.

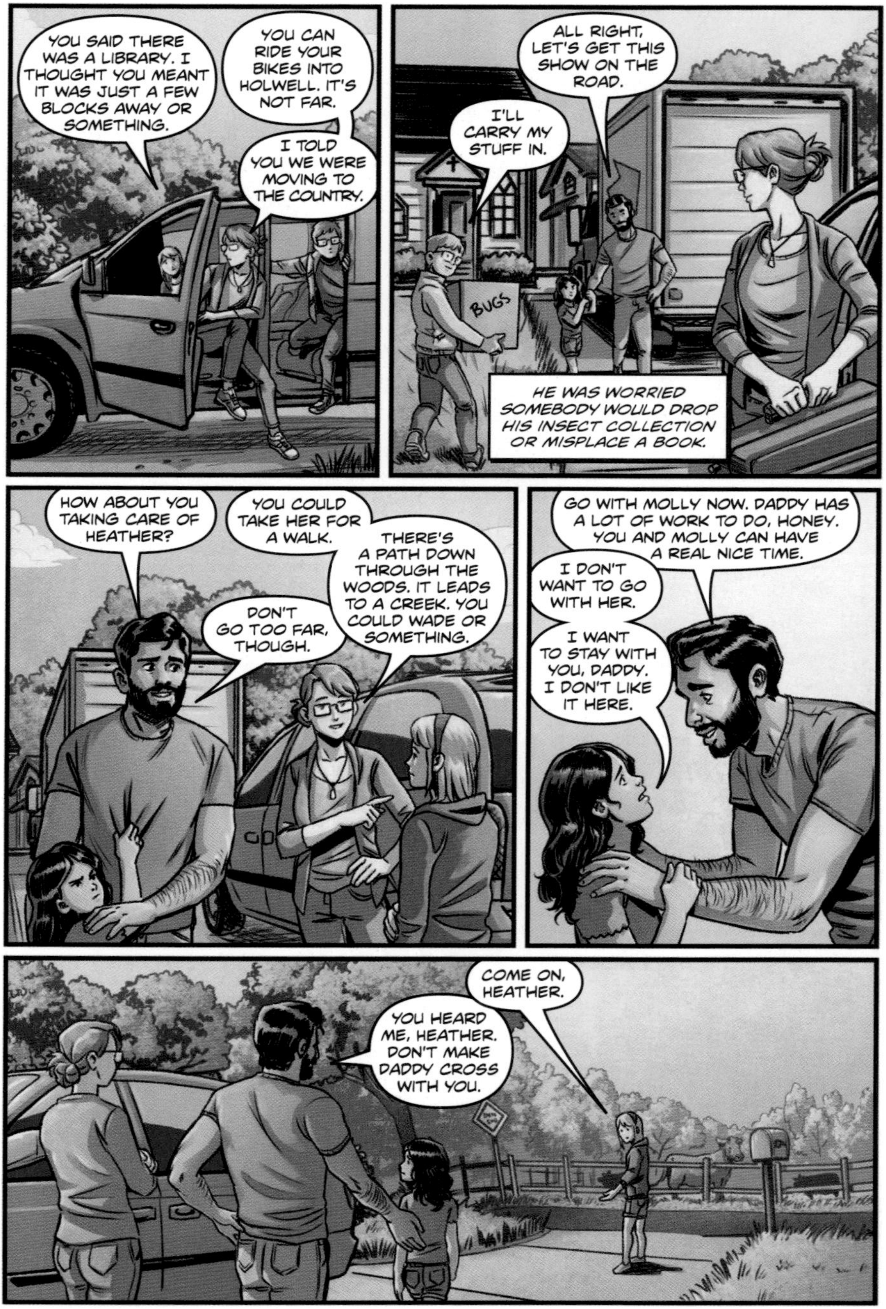
YOU SAID THERE WAS A LIBRARY. I THOUGHT YOU MEANT IT WAS JUST A FEW BLOCKS AWAY OR SOMETHING.
YOU CAN RIDE YOUR BIKES INTO HOLWELL. IT'S NOT FAR.
I TOLD YOU WE WERE MOVING TO THE COUNTRY.
ALL RIGHT, LET'S GET THIS SHOW ON THE ROAD.
I'LL CARRY MY STUFF IN.
BUGS
HE WAS WORRIED SOMEBODY WOULD DROP HIS INSECT COLLECTION OR MISPLACE A BOOK.
HOW ABOUT YOU TAKING CARE OF HEATHER?
YOU COULD TAKE HER FOR A WALK.
THERE'S A PATH DOWN THROUGH THE WOODS. IT LEADS TO A CREEK. YOU COULD WADE OR SOMETHING.
DON'T GO TOO FAR, THOUGH.
GO WITH MOLLY NOW. DADDY HAS A LOT OF WORK TO DO, HONEY. YOU AND MOLLY CAN HAVE A REAL NICE TIME.
I DON'T WANT TO GO WITH HER.
I WANT TO STAY WITH YOU, DADDY. I DON'T LIKE IT HERE.
COME ON, HEATHER.
YOU HEARD ME, HEATHER. DON'T MAKE DADDY CROSS WITH YOU.

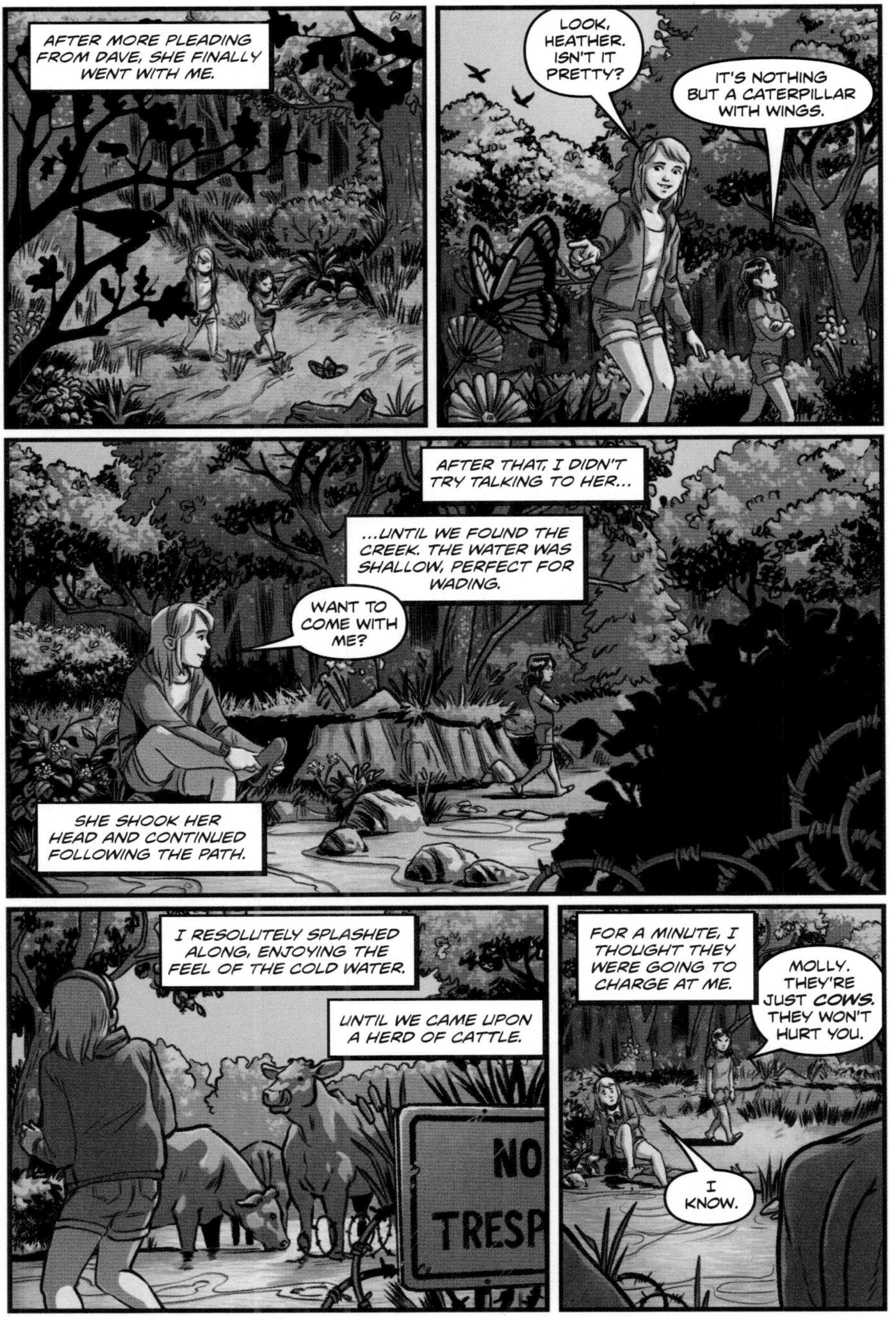
AFTER MORE PLEADING FROM DAVE, SHE FINALLY WENT WITH ME.
LOOK, HEATHER. ISN'T IT PRETTY?
IT'S NOTHING BUT A CATERPILLAR WITH WINGS.
AFTER THAT, I DIDN'T TRY TALKING TO HER...
...UNTIL WE FOUND THE CREEK. THE WATER WAS SHALLOW, PERFECT FOR WADING.
WANT TO COME WITH ME?
SHE SHOOK HER HEAD AND CONTINUED FOLLOWING THE PATH.
I RESOLUTELY SPLASHED ALONG, ENJOYING THE FEEL OF THE COLD WATER.
UNTIL WE CAME UPON A HERD OF CATTLE.
NO TRESP
FOR A MINUTE, I THOUGHT THEY WERE GOING TO CHARGE AT ME.
MOLLY. THEY'RE JUST COWS. THEY WON'T HURT YOU.
I KNOW.

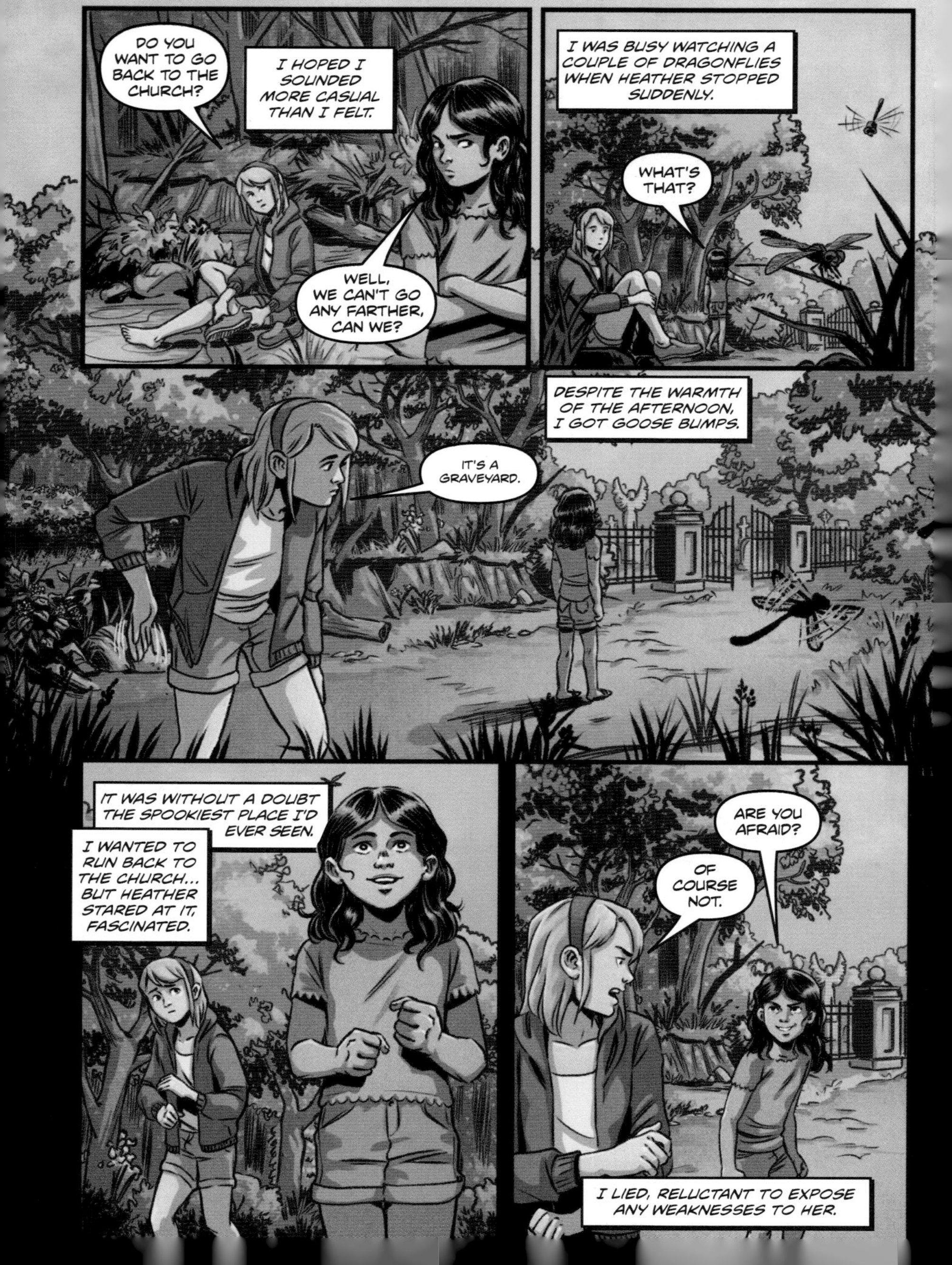
DO YOU WANT TO GO BACK TO THE CHURCH?
I HOPED I SOUNDED MORE CASUAL THAN I FELT.
WELL, WE CAN'T GO ANY FARTHER, CAN WE?
I WAS BUSY WATCHING A COUPLE OF DRAGONFLIES WHEN HEATHER STOPPED SUDDENLY.
WHAT'S THAT?
DESPITE THE WARMTH OF THE AFTERNOON, I GOT GOOSE BUMPS.
IT'S A GRAVEYARD.
IT WAS WITHOUT A DOUBT THE SPOOKIEST PLACE I'D EVER SEEN.
I WANTED TO RUN BACK TO THE CHURCH... BUT HEATHER STARED AT IT, FASCINATED.
ARE YOU AFRAID?
OF COURSE NOT.
I LIED, RELUCTANT TO EXPOSE ANY WEAKNESSES TO HER.

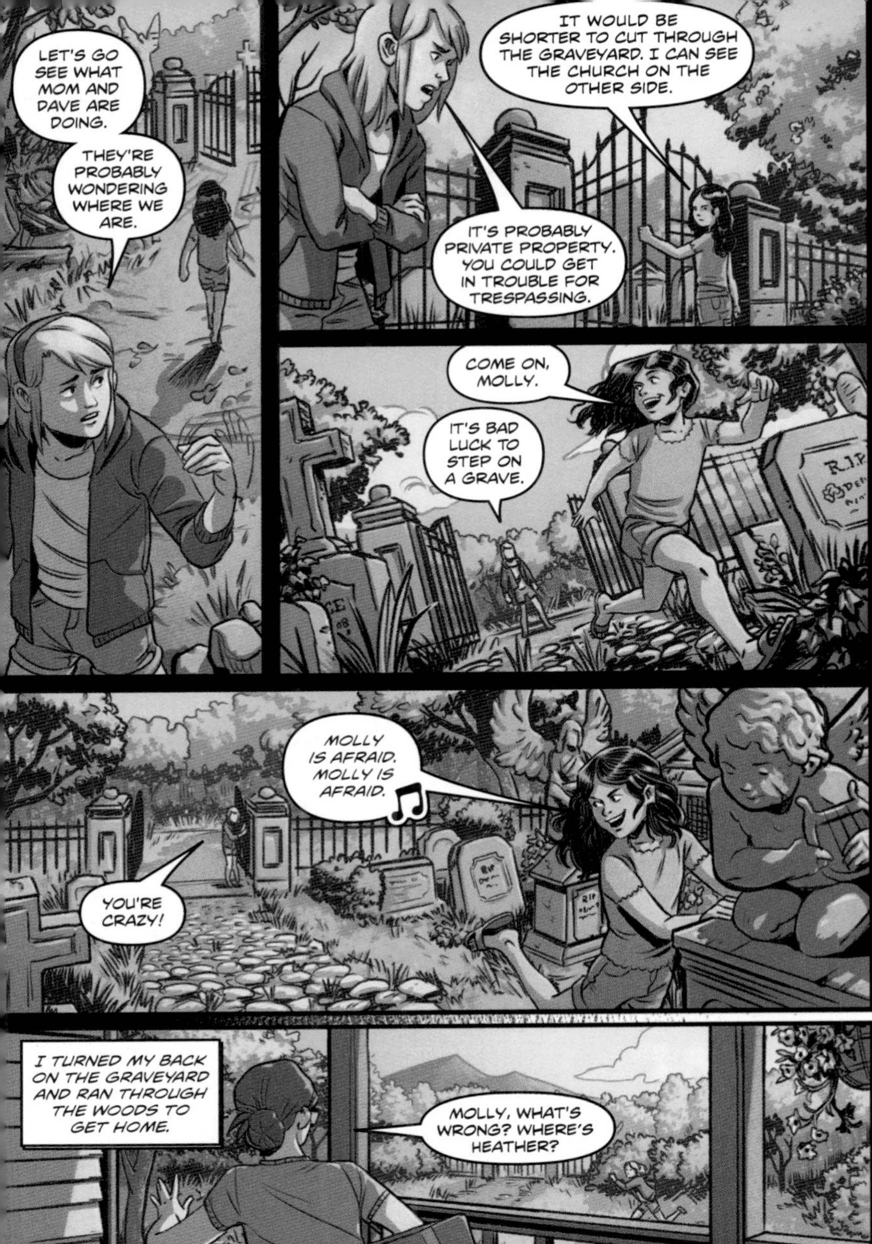
LET'S GO SEE WHAT MOM AND DAVE ARE DOING.
THEY'RE PROBABLY WONDERING WHERE WE ARE.
IT WOULD BE SHORTER TO CUT THROUGH THE GRAVEYARD. I CAN SEE THE CHURCH ON THE OTHER SIDE.
IT'S PROBABLY PRIVATE PROPERTY. YOU COULD GET IN TROUBLE FOR TRESPASSING.
COME ON, MOLLY.
IT'S BAD LUCK TO STEP ON A GRAVE.
R.I.P.
MOLLY IS AFRAID. MOLLY IS AFRAID.
YOU'RE CRAZY!
I TURNED MY BACK ON THE GRAVEYARD AND RAN THROUGH THE WOODS TO GET HOME.
MOLLY, WHAT'S WRONG? WHERE'S HEATHER?
KITCHEN

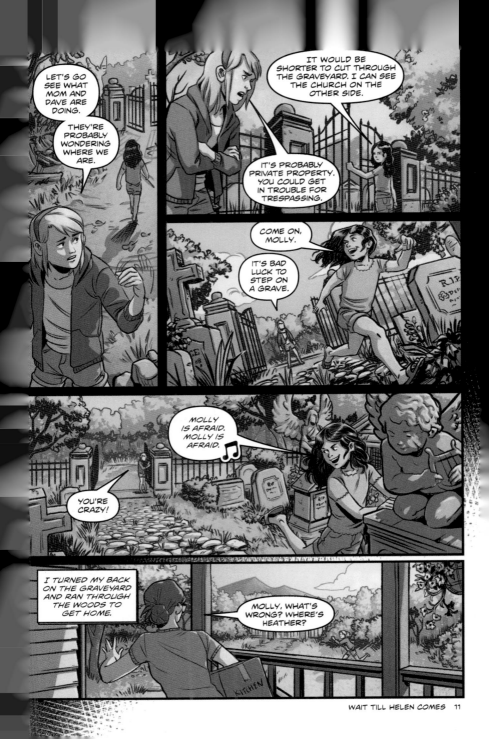

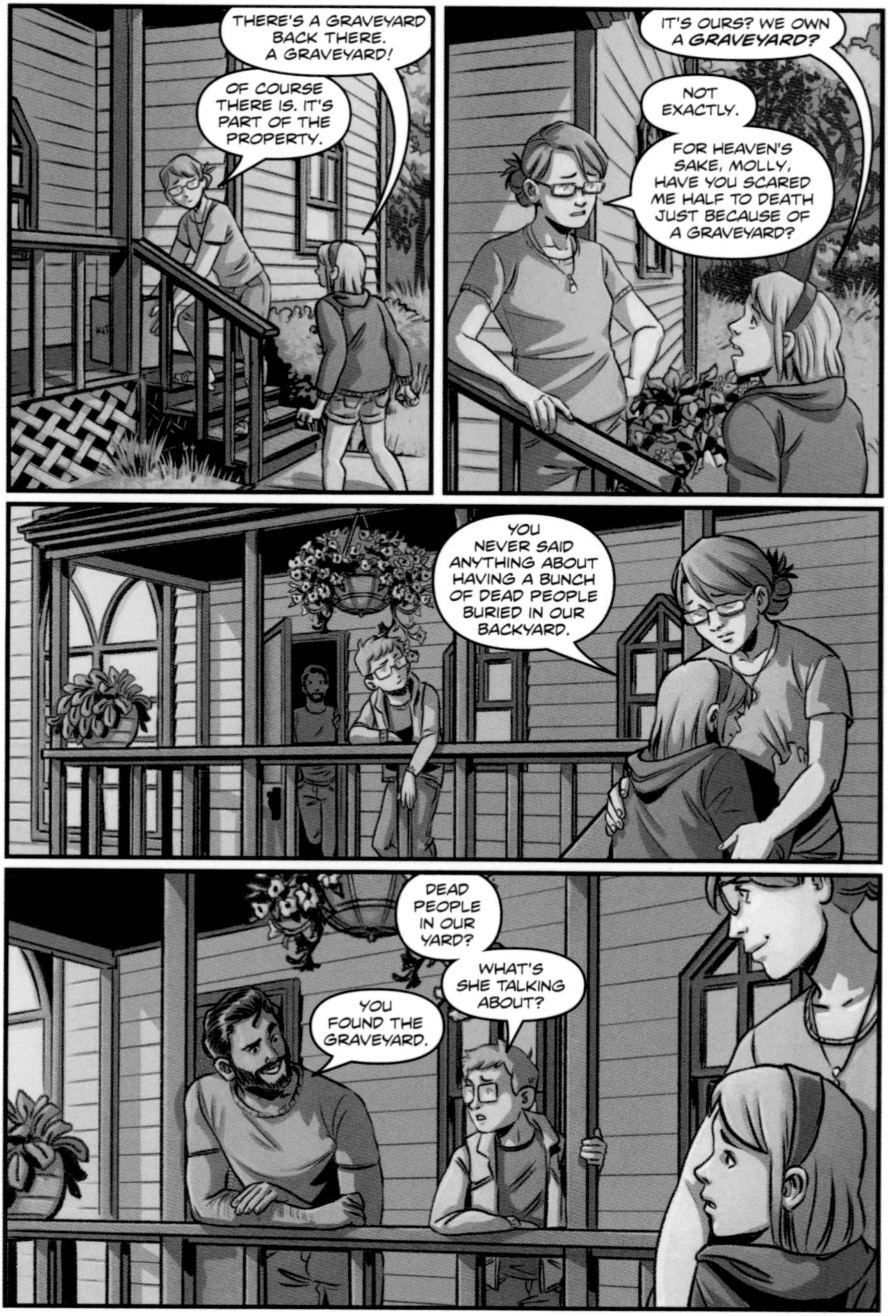
THERE'S A GRAVEYARD BACK THERE. A GRAVEYARD!
OF COURSE THERE IS. IT'S PART OF THE PROPERTY.
IT'S OURS? WE OWN A GRAVEYARD?
NOT EXACTLY.
FOR HEAVEN'S SAKE, MOLLY, HAVE YOU SCARED ME HALF TO DEATH JUST BECAUSE OF A GRAVEYARD?
YOU NEVER SAID ANYTHING ABOUT HAVING A BUNCH OF DEAD PEOPLE BURIED IN OUR BACKYARD.
DEAD PEOPLE IN OUR YARD?
WHAT'S SHE TALKING ABOUT?
YOU FOUND THE GRAVEYARD.

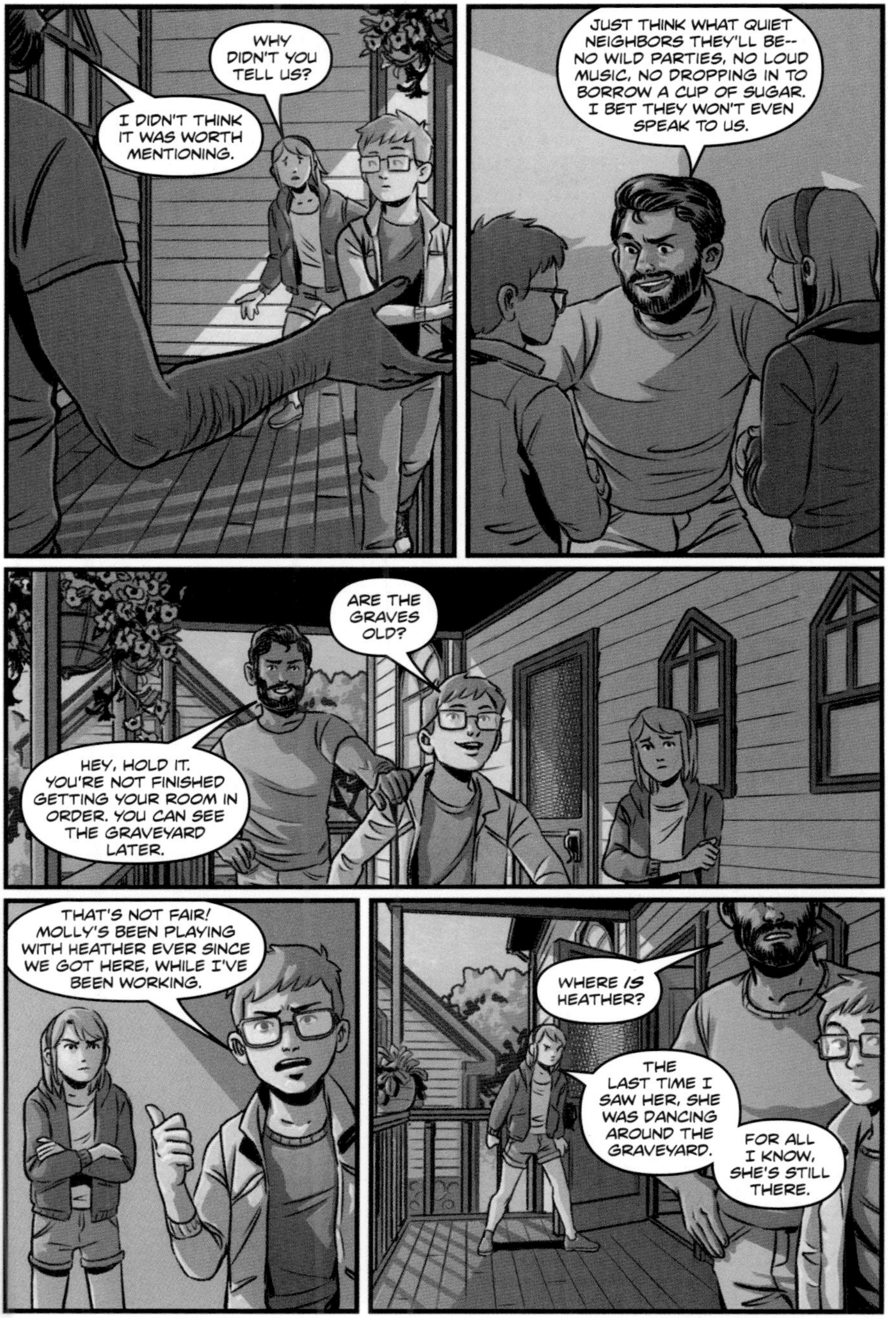
WHY DIDN'T YOU TELL US?
I DIDN'T THINK IT WAS WORTH MENTIONING.
JUST THINK WHAT QUIET NEIGHBORS THEY'LL BE-- NO WILD PARTIES, NO LOUD MUSIC, NO DROPPING IN TO BORROW A CUP OF SUGAR. I BET THEY WON'T EVEN SPEAK TO US.
ARE THE GRAVES OLD?
HEY, HOLD IT. YOU'RE NOT FINISHED GETTING YOUR ROOM IN ORDER. YOU CAN SEE THE GRAVEYARD LATER.
THAT'S NOT FAIR! MOLLY'S BEEN PLAYING WITH HEATHER EVER SINCE WE GOT HERE, WHILE I'VE BEEN WORKING.
WHERE *IS* HEATHER?
THE LAST TIME I SAW HER, SHE WAS DANCING AROUND THE GRAVEYARD.
FOR ALL I KNOW, SHE'S STILL THERE.

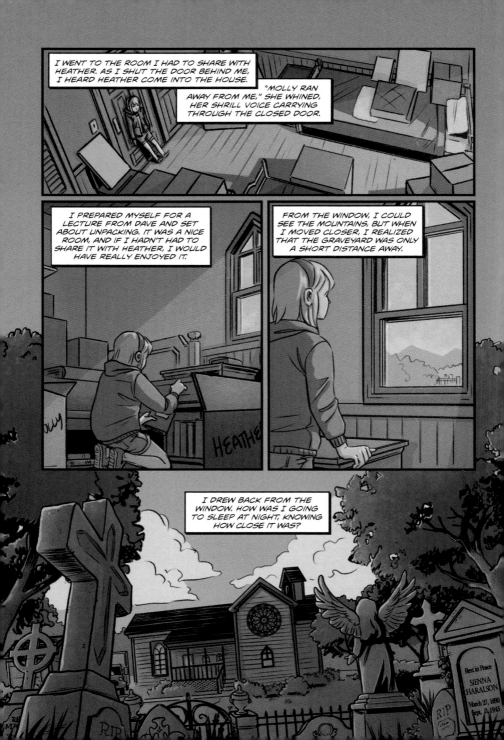

I WENT TO THE ROOM I HAD TO SHARE WITH HEATHER. AS I SHUT THE DOOR BEHIND ME, I HEARD HEATHER COME INTO THE HOUSE.

"MOLLY RAN AWAY FROM ME," SHE WHINED, HER SHRILL VOICE CARRYING THROUGH THE CLOSED DOOR.

I PREPARED MYSELF FOR A LECTURE FROM DAVE AND SET ABOUT UNPACKING. IT WAS A NICE ROOM, AND IF I HADN'T HAD TO SHARE IT WITH HEATHER, I WOULD HAVE REALLY ENJOYED IT.

FROM THE WINDOW, I COULD SEE THE MOUNTAINS, BUT WHEN I MOVED CLOSER, I REALIZED THAT THE GRAVEYARD WAS ONLY A SHORT DISTANCE AWAY.

I DREW BACK FROM THE WINDOW. HOW WAS I GOING TO SLEEP AT NIGHT, KNOWING HOW CLOSE IT WAS?

Rest in Peace
SIENNA
HARALSON
March 27, 1890
Sept. 8, 1941

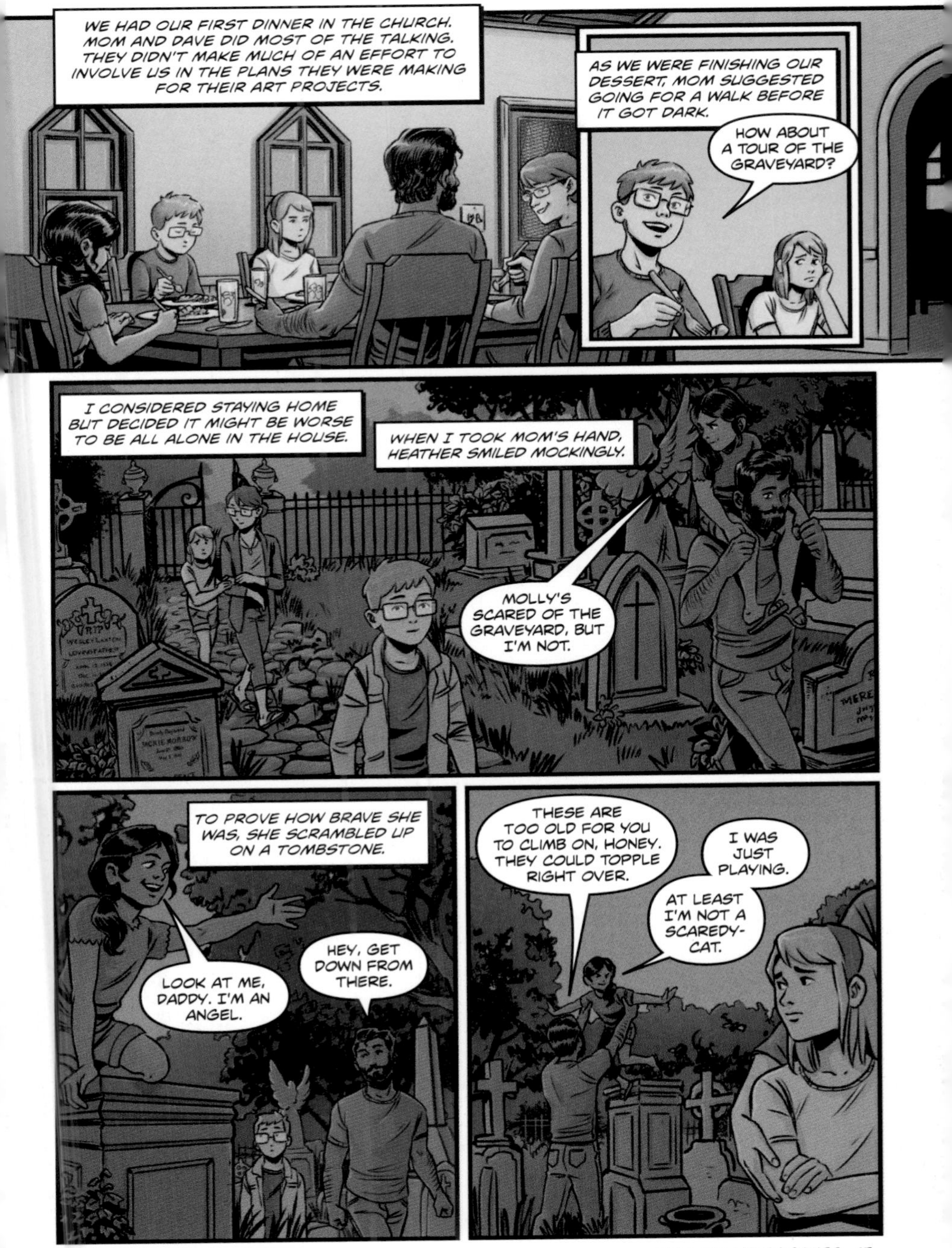
WE HAD OUR FIRST DINNER IN THE CHURCH. MOM AND DAVE DID MOST OF THE TALKING. THEY DIDN'T MAKE MUCH OF AN EFFORT TO INVOLVE US IN THE PLANS THEY WERE MAKING FOR THEIR ART PROJECTS.
AS WE WERE FINISHING OUR DESSERT, MOM SUGGESTED GOING FOR A WALK BEFORE IT GOT DARK.
HOW ABOUT A TOUR OF THE GRAVEYARD?
I CONSIDERED STAYING HOME BUT DECIDED IT MIGHT BE WORSE TO BE ALL ALONE IN THE HOUSE.
WHEN I TOOK MOM'S HAND, HEATHER SMILED MOCKINGLY.
MOLLY'S SCARED OF THE GRAVEYARD, BUT I'M NOT.
TO PROVE HOW BRAVE SHE WAS, SHE SCRAMBLED UP ON A TOMBSTONE.
LOOK AT ME, DADDY. I'M AN ANGEL.
HEY, GET DOWN FROM THERE.
THESE ARE TOO OLD FOR YOU TO CLIMB ON, HONEY. THEY COULD TOPPLE RIGHT OVER.
I WAS JUST PLAYING.
AT LEAST I'M NOT A SCAREDY-CAT.

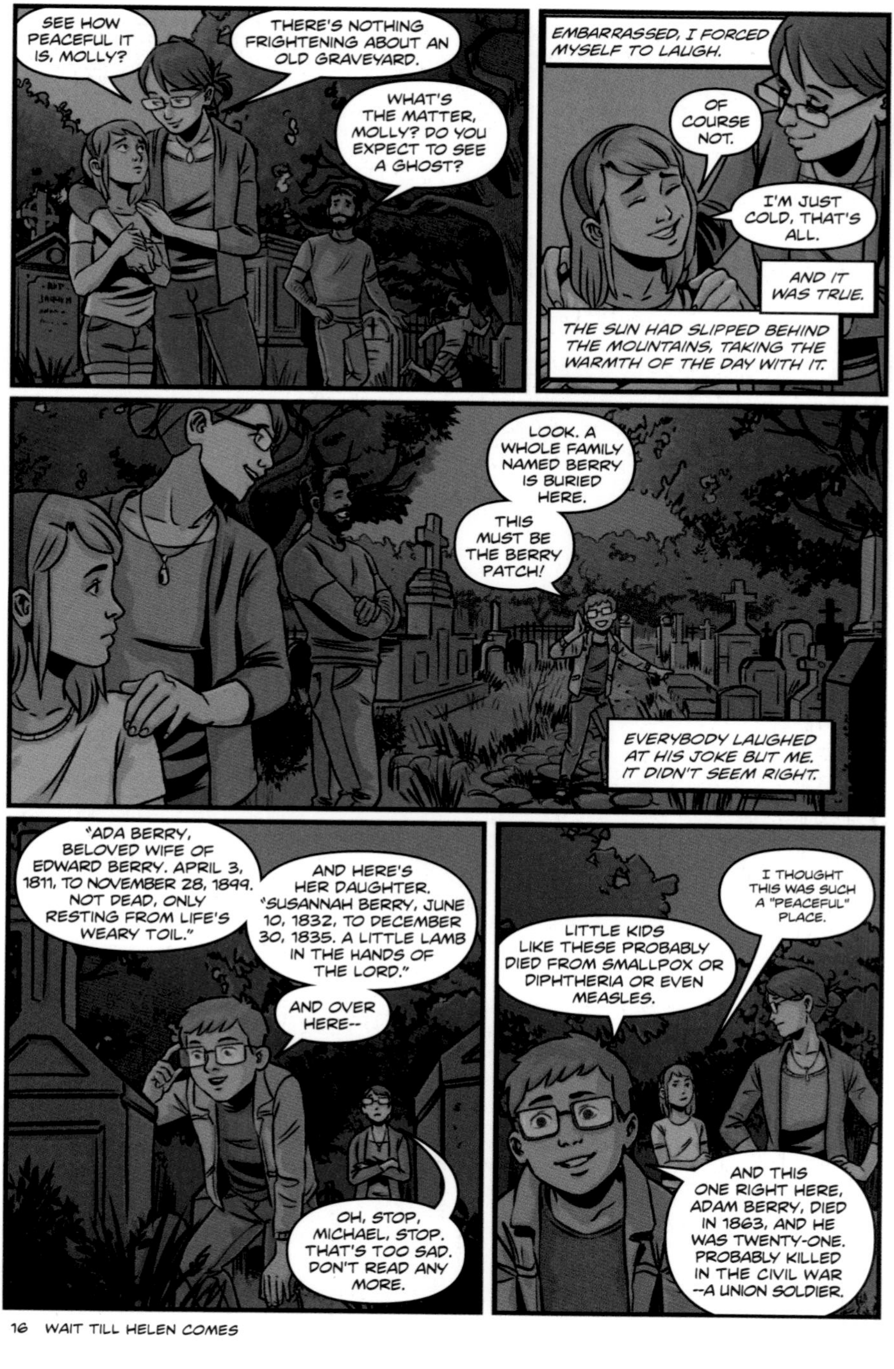
SEE HOW PEACEFUL IT IS, MOLLY?
THERE'S NOTHING FRIGHTENING ABOUT AN OLD GRAVEYARD.
WHAT'S THE MATTER, MOLLY? DO YOU EXPECT TO SEE A GHOST?
EMBARRASSED, I FORCED MYSELF TO LAUGH.
OF COURSE NOT.
I'M JUST COLD, THAT'S ALL.
AND IT WAS TRUE.
THE SUN HAD SLIPPED BEHIND THE MOUNTAINS, TAKING THE WARMTH OF THE DAY WITH IT.
LOOK. A WHOLE FAMILY NAMED BERRY IS BURIED HERE.
THIS MUST BE THE BERRY PATCH!
EVERYBODY LAUGHED AT HIS JOKE BUT ME. IT DIDN'T SEEM RIGHT.
"ADA BERRY, BELOVED WIFE OF EDWARD BERRY. APRIL 3, 1811, TO NOVEMBER 28, 1899. NOT DEAD, ONLY RESTING FROM LIFE'S WEARY TOIL."
AND HERE'S HER DAUGHTER. "SUSANNAH BERRY, JUNE 10, 1832, TO DECEMBER 30, 1835. A LITTLE LAMB IN THE HANDS OF THE LORD."
AND OVER HERE--
OH, STOP, MICHAEL, STOP. THAT'S TOO SAD. DON'T READ ANY MORE.
LITTLE KIDS LIKE THESE PROBABLY DIED FROM SMALLPOX OR DIPHTHERIA OR EVEN MEASLES.
I THOUGHT THIS WAS SUCH A "PEACEFUL" PLACE.
AND THIS ONE RIGHT HERE, ADAM BERRY, DIED IN 1863, AND HE WAS TWENTY-ONE. PROBABLY KILLED IN THE CIVIL WAR --A UNION SOLDIER.

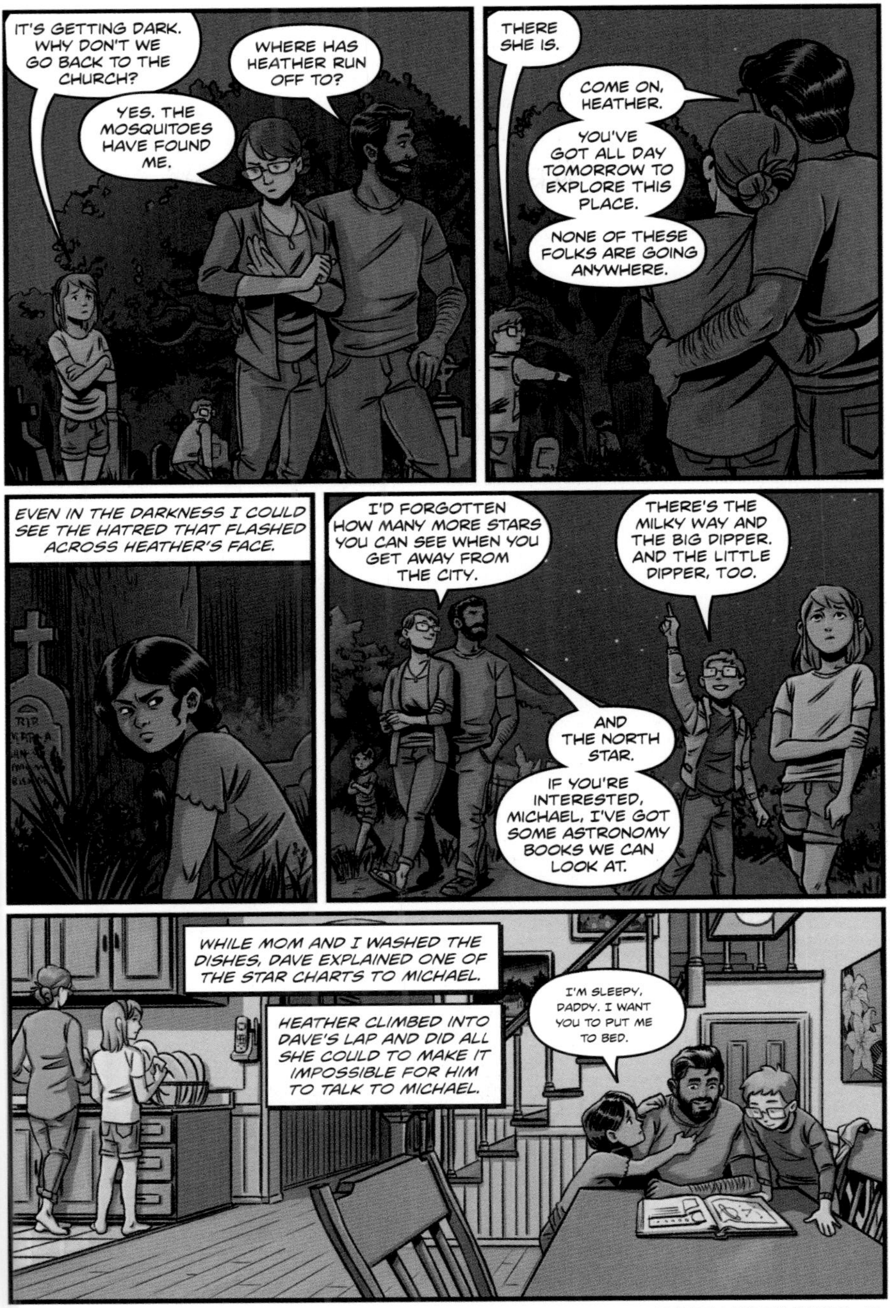
IT'S GETTING DARK. WHY DON'T WE GO BACK TO THE CHURCH?
WHERE HAS HEATHER RUN OFF TO?
YES. THE MOSQUITOES HAVE FOUND ME.
THERE SHE IS.
COME ON, HEATHER.
YOU'VE GOT ALL DAY TOMORROW TO EXPLORE THIS PLACE.
NONE OF THESE FOLKS ARE GOING ANYWHERE.
EVEN IN THE DARKNESS I COULD SEE THE HATRED THAT FLASHED ACROSS HEATHER'S FACE.
I'D FORGOTTEN HOW MANY MORE STARS YOU CAN SEE WHEN YOU GET AWAY FROM THE CITY.
THERE'S THE MILKY WAY AND THE BIG DIPPER. AND THE LITTLE DIPPER, TOO.
AND THE NORTH STAR.
IF YOU'RE INTERESTED, MICHAEL, I'VE GOT SOME ASTRONOMY BOOKS WE CAN LOOK AT.
WHILE MOM AND I WASHED THE DISHES, DAVE EXPLAINED ONE OF THE STAR CHARTS TO MICHAEL.
HEATHER CLIMBED INTO DAVE'S LAP AND DID ALL SHE COULD TO MAKE IT IMPOSSIBLE FOR HIM TO TALK TO MICHAEL.
I'M SLEEPY, DADDY. I WANT YOU TO PUT ME TO BED.

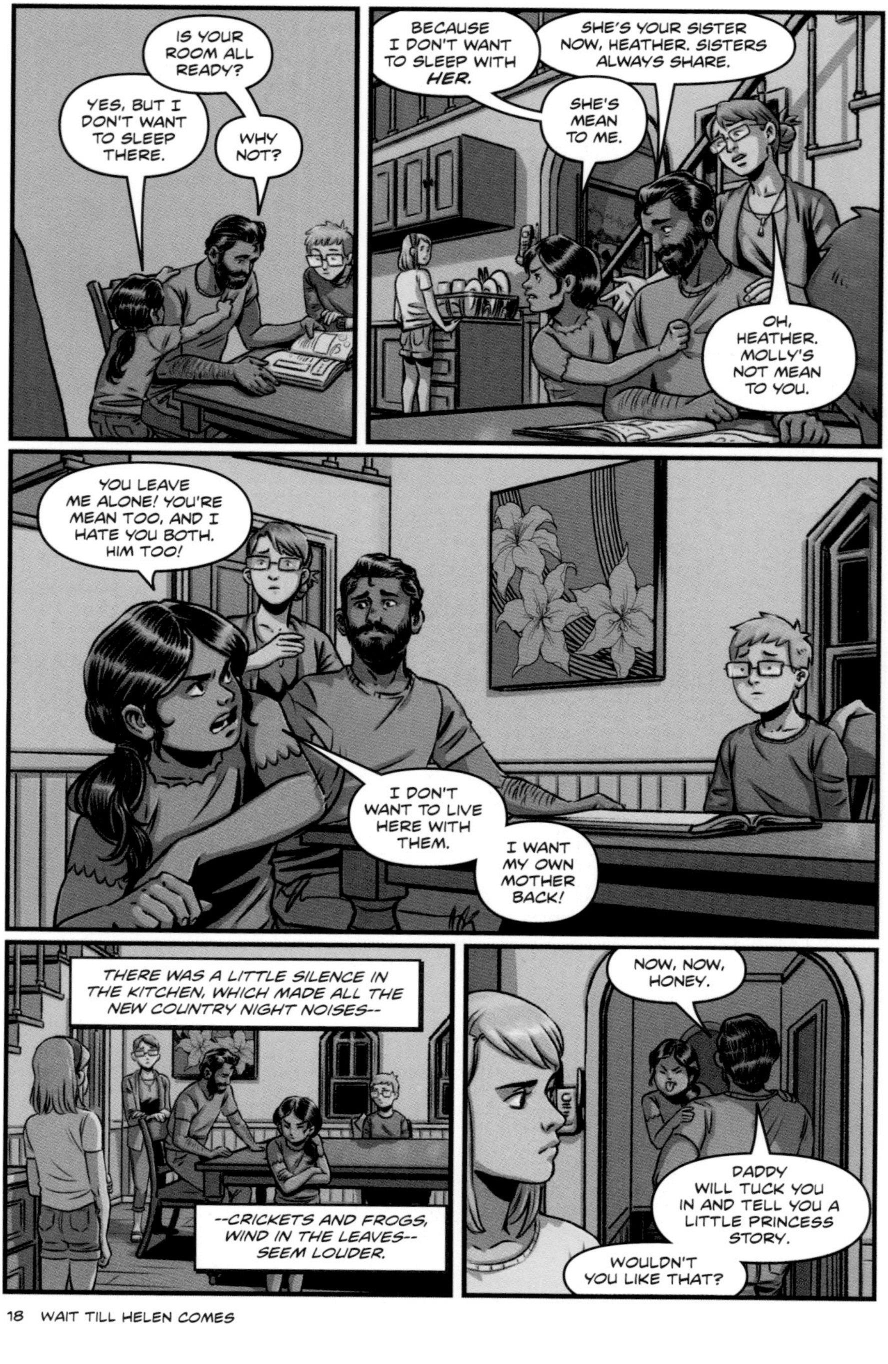
IS YOUR ROOM ALL READY?
YES, BUT I DON'T WANT TO SLEEP THERE.
WHY NOT?
BECAUSE I DON'T WANT TO SLEEP WITH HER.
SHE'S YOUR SISTER NOW, HEATHER. SISTERS ALWAYS SHARE.
SHE'S MEAN TO ME.
OH, HEATHER. MOLLY'S NOT MEAN TO YOU.
YOU LEAVE ME ALONE! YOU'RE MEAN TOO, AND I HATE YOU BOTH. HIM TOO!
I DON'T WANT TO LIVE HERE WITH THEM.
I WANT MY OWN MOTHER BACK!
THERE WAS A LITTLE SILENCE IN THE KITCHEN, WHICH MADE ALL THE NEW COUNTRY NIGHT NOISES--
--CRICKETS AND FROGS, WIND IN THE LEAVES-- SEEM LOUDER.
NOW, NOW, HONEY.
DADDY WILL TUCK YOU IN AND TELL YOU A LITTLE PRINCESS STORY.
WOULDN'T YOU LIKE THAT?

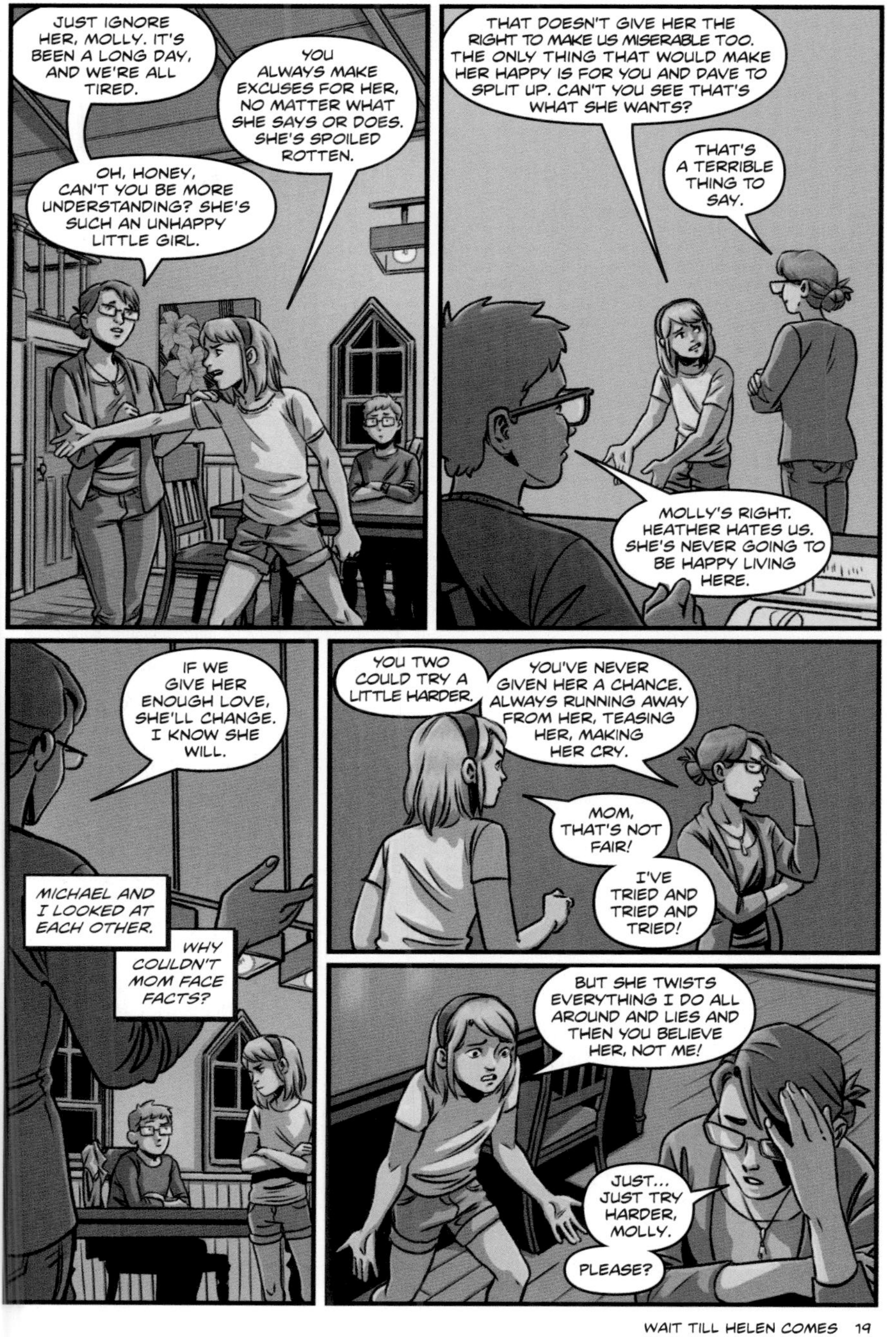
JUST IGNORE HER, MOLLY. IT'S BEEN A LONG DAY, AND WE'RE ALL TIRED.
OH, HONEY, CAN'T YOU BE MORE UNDERSTANDING? SHE'S SUCH AN UNHAPPY LITTLE GIRL.
YOU ALWAYS MAKE EXCUSES FOR HER, NO MATTER WHAT SHE SAYS OR DOES. SHE'S SPOILED ROTTEN.
THAT DOESN'T GIVE HER THE RIGHT TO MAKE US MISERABLE TOO. THE ONLY THING THAT WOULD MAKE HER HAPPY IS FOR YOU AND DAVE TO SPLIT UP. CAN'T YOU SEE THAT'S WHAT SHE WANTS?
THAT'S A TERRIBLE THING TO SAY.
MOLLY'S RIGHT. HEATHER HATES US. SHE'S NEVER GOING TO BE HAPPY LIVING HERE.
IF WE GIVE HER ENOUGH LOVE, SHE'LL CHANGE. I KNOW SHE WILL.
MICHAEL AND I LOOKED AT EACH OTHER.
WHY COULDN'T MOM FACE FACTS?
YOU TWO COULD TRY A LITTLE HARDER.
YOU'VE NEVER GIVEN HER A CHANCE. ALWAYS RUNNING AWAY FROM HER, TEASING HER, MAKING HER CRY.
MOM, THAT'S NOT FAIR!
I'VE TRIED AND TRIED AND TRIED!
BUT SHE TWISTS EVERYTHING I DO ALL AROUND AND LIES AND THEN YOU BELIEVE HER, NOT ME!
JUST... JUST TRY HARDER, MOLLY.
PLEASE?

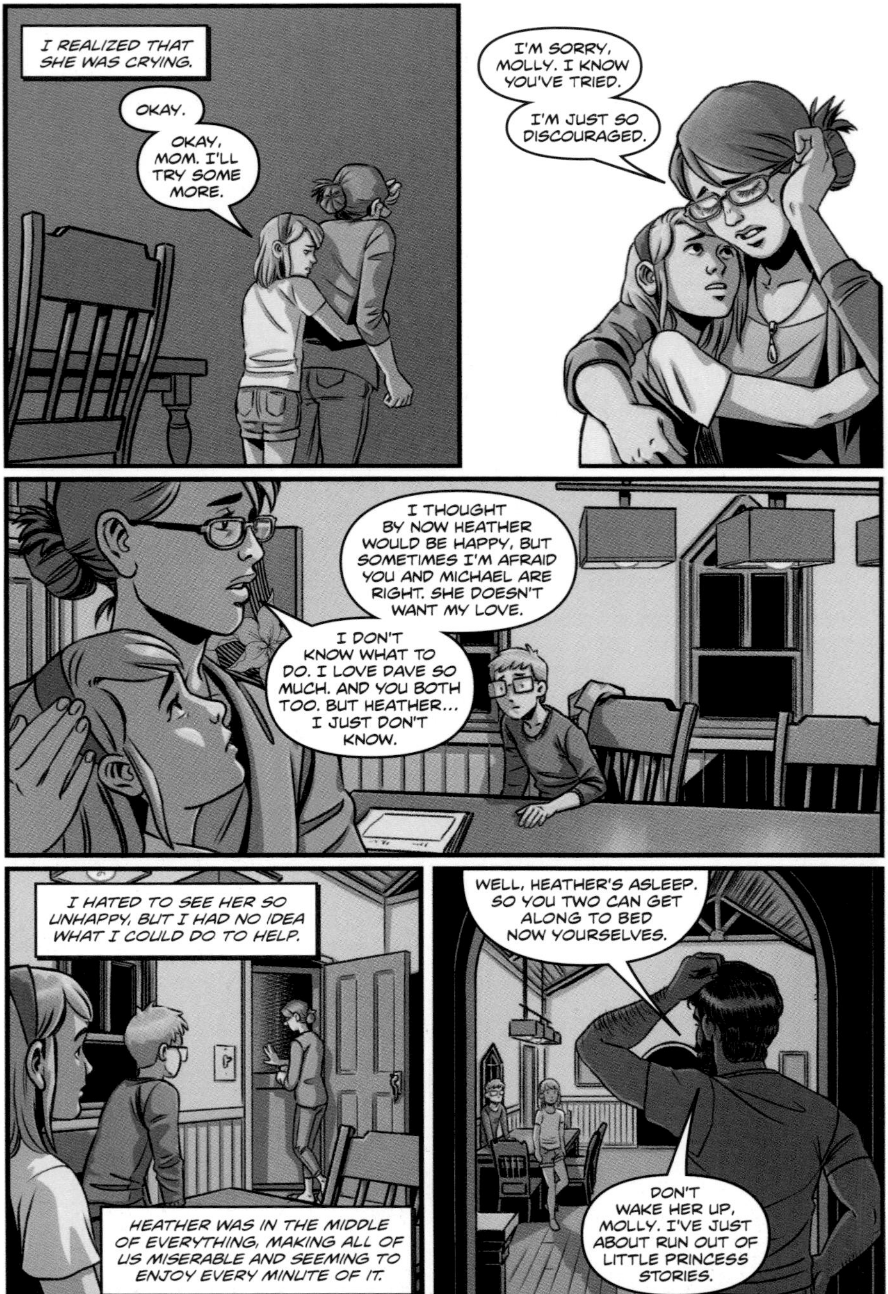
I REALIZED THAT SHE WAS CRYING.
OKAY.
OKAY, MOM. I'LL TRY SOME MORE.
I'M SORRY, MOLLY. I KNOW YOU'VE TRIED.
I'M JUST SO DISCOURAGED.
I THOUGHT BY NOW HEATHER WOULD BE HAPPY, BUT SOMETIMES I'M AFRAID YOU AND MICHAEL ARE RIGHT. SHE DOESN'T WANT MY LOVE.
I DON'T KNOW WHAT TO DO. I LOVE DAVE SO MUCH. AND YOU BOTH TOO. BUT HEATHER... I JUST DON'T KNOW.
I HATED TO SEE HER SO UNHAPPY, BUT I HAD NO IDEA WHAT I COULD DO TO HELP.
HEATHER WAS IN THE MIDDLE OF EVERYTHING, MAKING ALL OF US MISERABLE AND SEEMING TO ENJOY EVERY MINUTE OF IT.
WELL, HEATHER'S ASLEEP. SO YOU TWO CAN GET ALONG TO BED NOW YOURSELVES.
DON'T WAKE HER UP, MOLLY. I'VE JUST ABOUT RUN OUT OF LITTLE PRINCESS STORIES.

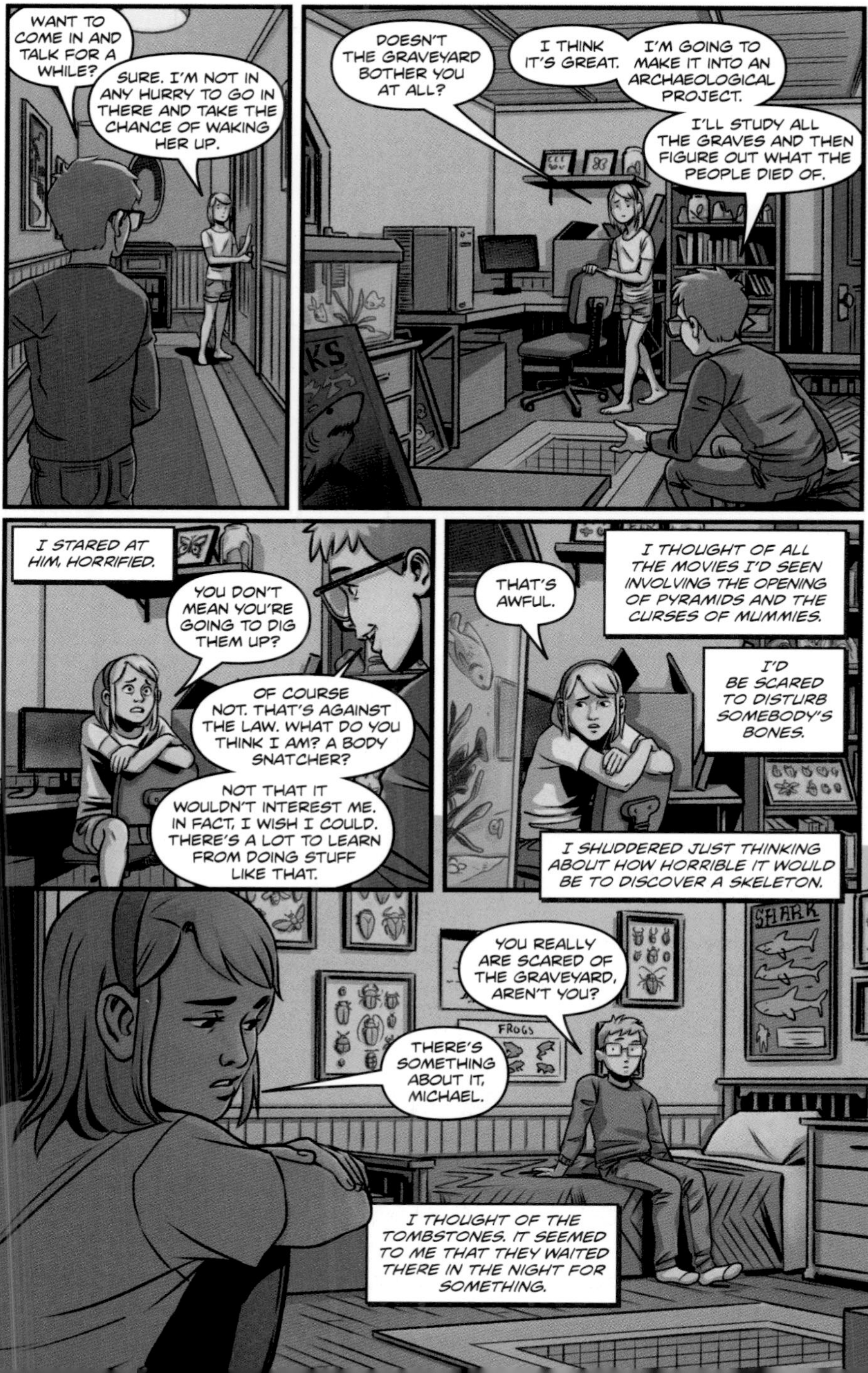
WANT TO COME IN AND TALK FOR A WHILE?
SURE. I'M NOT IN ANY HURRY TO GO IN THERE AND TAKE THE CHANCE OF WAKING HER UP.
DOESN'T THE GRAVEYARD BOTHER YOU AT ALL?
I THINK IT'S GREAT.
I'M GOING TO MAKE IT INTO AN ARCHAEOLOGICAL PROJECT.
I'LL STUDY ALL THE GRAVES AND THEN FIGURE OUT WHAT THE PEOPLE DIED OF.
I STARED AT HIM, HORRIFIED.
YOU DON'T MEAN YOU'RE GOING TO DIG THEM UP?
OF COURSE NOT. THAT'S AGAINST THE LAW. WHAT DO YOU THINK I AM? A BODY SNATCHER?
NOT THAT IT WOULDN'T INTEREST ME. IN FACT, I WISH I COULD. THERE'S A LOT TO LEARN FROM DOING STUFF LIKE THAT.
THAT'S AWFUL.
I THOUGHT OF ALL THE MOVIES I'D SEEN INVOLVING THE OPENING OF PYRAMIDS AND THE CURSES OF MUMMIES.
I'D BE SCARED TO DISTURB SOMEBODY'S BONES.
I SHUDDERED JUST THINKING ABOUT HOW HORRIBLE IT WOULD BE TO DISCOVER A SKELETON.
SHARK
FROGS
YOU REALLY ARE SCARED OF THE GRAVEYARD, AREN'T YOU?
THERE'S SOMETHING ABOUT IT, MICHAEL.
I THOUGHT OF THE TOMBSTONES. IT SEEMED TO ME THAT THEY WAITED THERE IN THE NIGHT FOR SOMETHING.

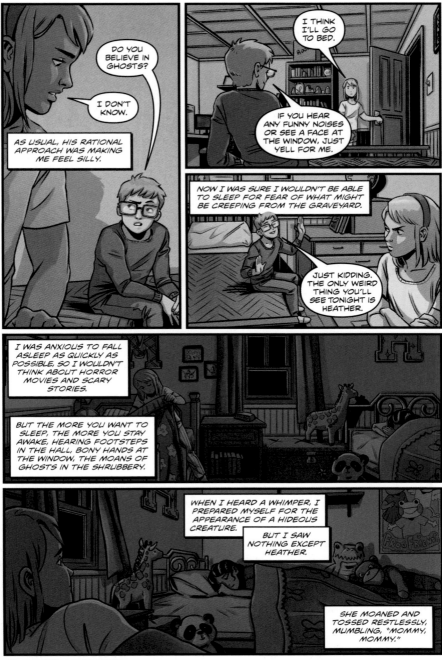

DO YOU BELIEVE IN GHOSTS?

I DON'T KNOW.

AS USUAL, HIS RATIONAL APPROACH WAS MAKING ME FEEL SILLY.

I THINK I'LL GO TO BED.

IF YOU HEAR ANY FUNNY NOISES OR SEE A FACE AT THE WINDOW, JUST YELL FOR ME.

NOW I WAS SURE I WOULDN'T BE ABLE TO SLEEP FOR FEAR OF WHAT MIGHT BE CREEPING FROM THE GRAVEYARD.

JUST KIDDING. THE ONLY WEIRD THING YOU'LL SEE TONIGHT IS HEATHER.

I WAS ANXIOUS TO FALL ASLEEP AS QUICKLY AS POSSIBLE, SO I WOULDN'T THINK ABOUT HORROR MOVIES AND SCARY STORIES.

BUT THE MORE YOU WANT TO SLEEP, THE MORE YOU STAY AWAKE, HEARING FOOTSTEPS IN THE HALL, BONY HANDS AT THE WINDOW, THE MOANS OF GHOSTS IN THE SHRUBBERY.

WHEN I HEARD A WHIMPER, I PREPARED MYSELF FOR THE APPEARANCE OF A HIDEOUS CREATURE.

BUT I SAW NOTHING EXCEPT HEATHER.

SHE MOANED AND TOSSED RESTLESSLY, MUMBLING, "MOMMY, MOMMY."

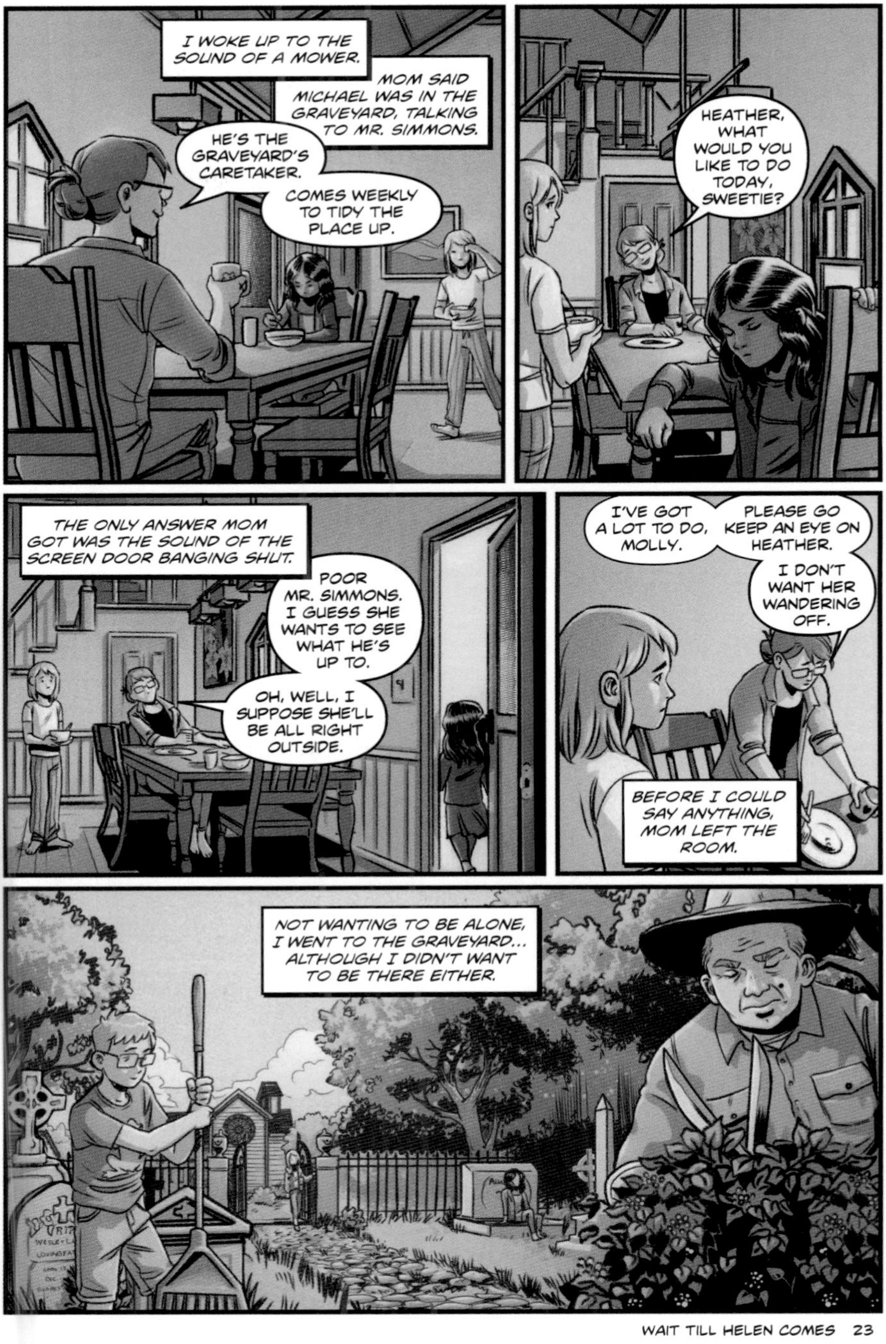
I WOKE UP TO THE SOUND OF A MOWER.
MOM SAID MICHAEL WAS IN THE GRAVEYARD, TALKING TO MR. SIMMONS.
HE'S THE GRAVEYARD'S CARETAKER.
COMES WEEKLY TO TIDY THE PLACE UP.
HEATHER, WHAT WOULD YOU LIKE TO DO TODAY, SWEETIE?
THE ONLY ANSWER MOM GOT WAS THE SOUND OF THE SCREEN DOOR BANGING SHUT.
POOR MR. SIMMONS. I GUESS SHE WANTS TO SEE WHAT HE'S UP TO.
OH, WELL, I SUPPOSE SHE'LL BE ALL RIGHT OUTSIDE.
I'VE GOT A LOT TO DO, MOLLY.
PLEASE GO KEEP AN EYE ON HEATHER.
I DON'T WANT HER WANDERING OFF.
BEFORE I COULD SAY ANYTHING, MOM LEFT THE ROOM.
NOT WANTING TO BE ALONE, I WENT TO THE GRAVEYARD... ALTHOUGH I DIDN'T WANT TO BE THERE EITHER.

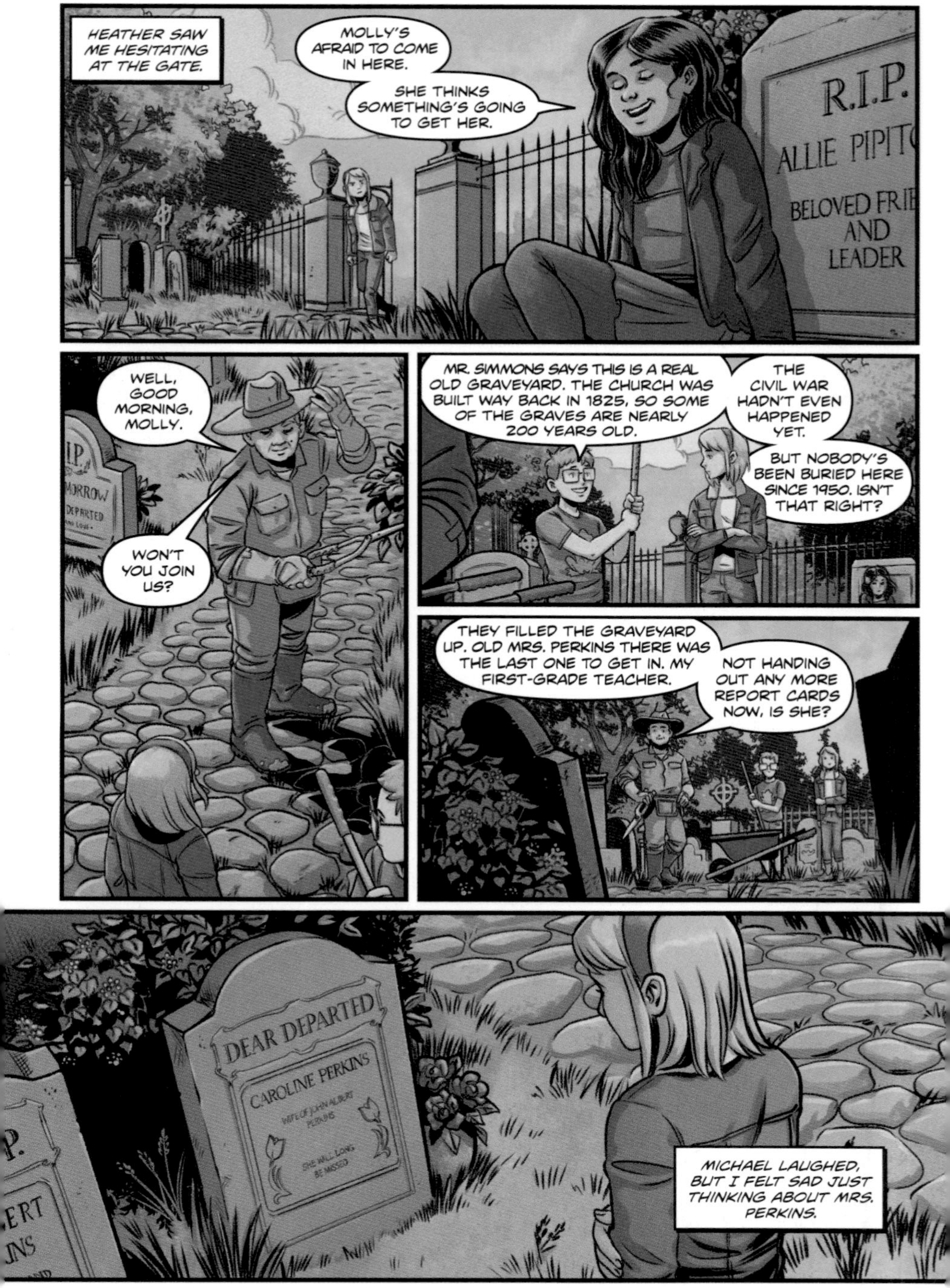
HEATHER SAW ME HESITATING AT THE GATE.
MOLLY'S AFRAID TO COME IN HERE.
SHE THINKS SOMETHING'S GOING TO GET HER.
R.I.P.
AND
LEADER
WELL, GOOD MORNING, MOLLY.
WON'T YOU JOIN US?
MR. SIMMONS SAYS THIS IS A REAL OLD GRAVEYARD. THE CHURCH WAS BUILT WAY BACK IN 1825, SO SOME OF THE GRAVES ARE NEARLY 200 YEARS OLD.
THE CIVIL WAR HADN'T EVEN HAPPENED YET.
BUT NOBODY'S BEEN BURIED HERE SINCE 1950. ISN'T THAT RIGHT?
THEY FILLED THE GRAVEYARD UP. OLD MRS. PERKINS THERE WAS THE LAST ONE TO GET IN. MY FIRST-GRADE TEACHER.
NOT HANDING OUT ANY MORE REPORT CARDS NOW, IS SHE?
DEAR DEPARTED
CAROLINE PERKINS
MICHAEL LAUGHED, BUT I FELT SAD JUST THINKING ABOUT MRS. PERKINS.

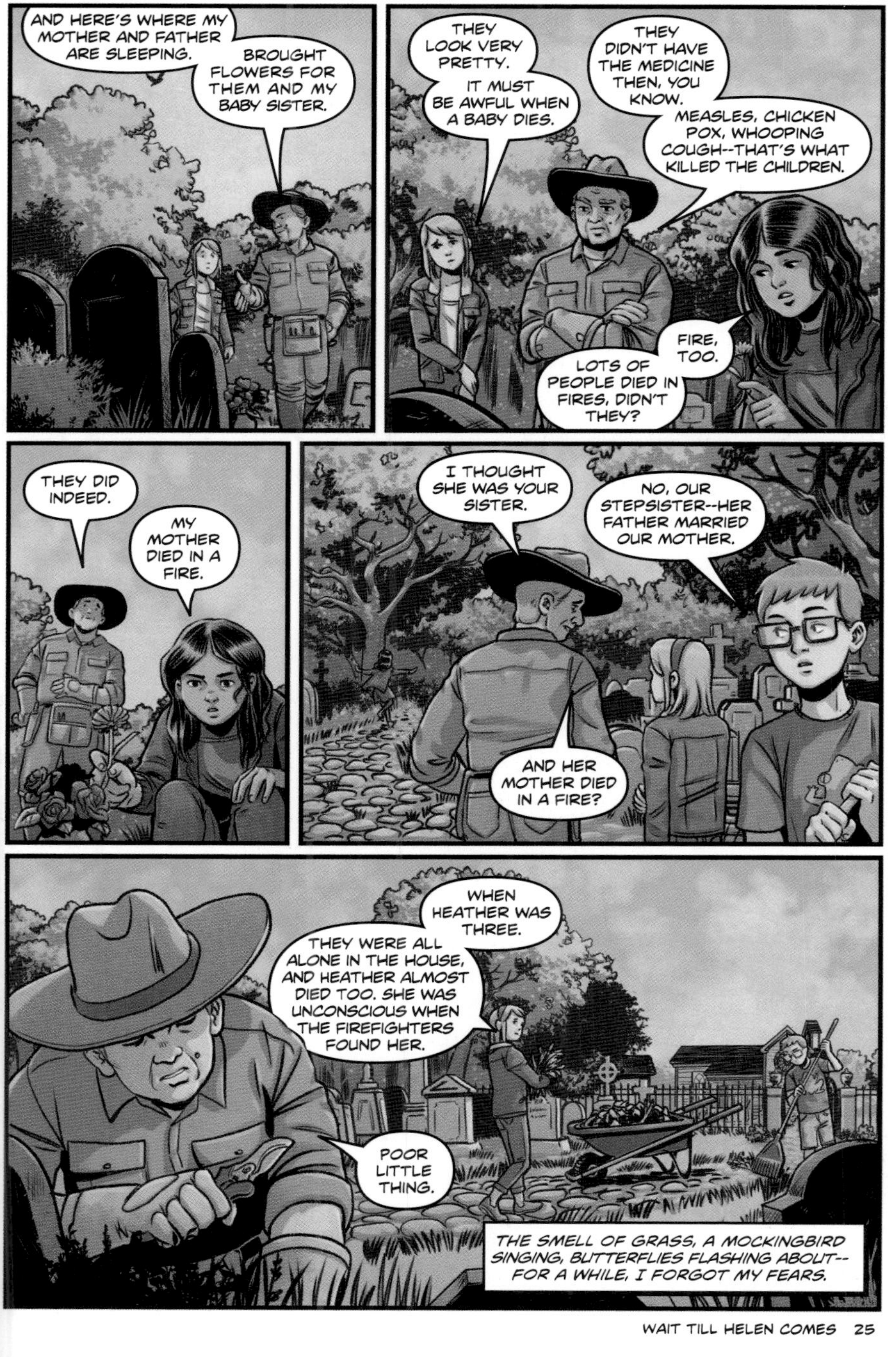
AND HERE'S WHERE MY MOTHER AND FATHER ARE SLEEPING.
BROUGHT FLOWERS FOR THEM AND MY BABY SISTER.
THEY LOOK VERY PRETTY.
IT MUST BE AWFUL WHEN A BABY DIES.
THEY DIDN'T HAVE THE MEDICINE THEN, YOU KNOW.
MEASLES, CHICKEN POX, WHOOPING COUGH--THAT'S WHAT KILLED THE CHILDREN.
FIRE, TOO.
LOTS OF PEOPLE DIED IN FIRES, DIDN'T THEY?
THEY DID INDEED.
MY MOTHER DIED IN A FIRE.
I THOUGHT SHE WAS YOUR SISTER.
NO, OUR STEPSISTER--HER FATHER MARRIED OUR MOTHER.
AND HER MOTHER DIED IN A FIRE?
WHEN HEATHER WAS THREE.
THEY WERE ALL ALONE IN THE HOUSE, AND HEATHER ALMOST DIED TOO. SHE WAS UNCONSCIOUS WHEN THE FIREFIGHTERS FOUND HER.
POOR LITTLE THING.
THE SMELL OF GRASS, A MOCKINGBIRD SINGING, BUTTERFLIES FLASHING ABOUT--FOR A WHILE, I FORGOT MY FEARS.

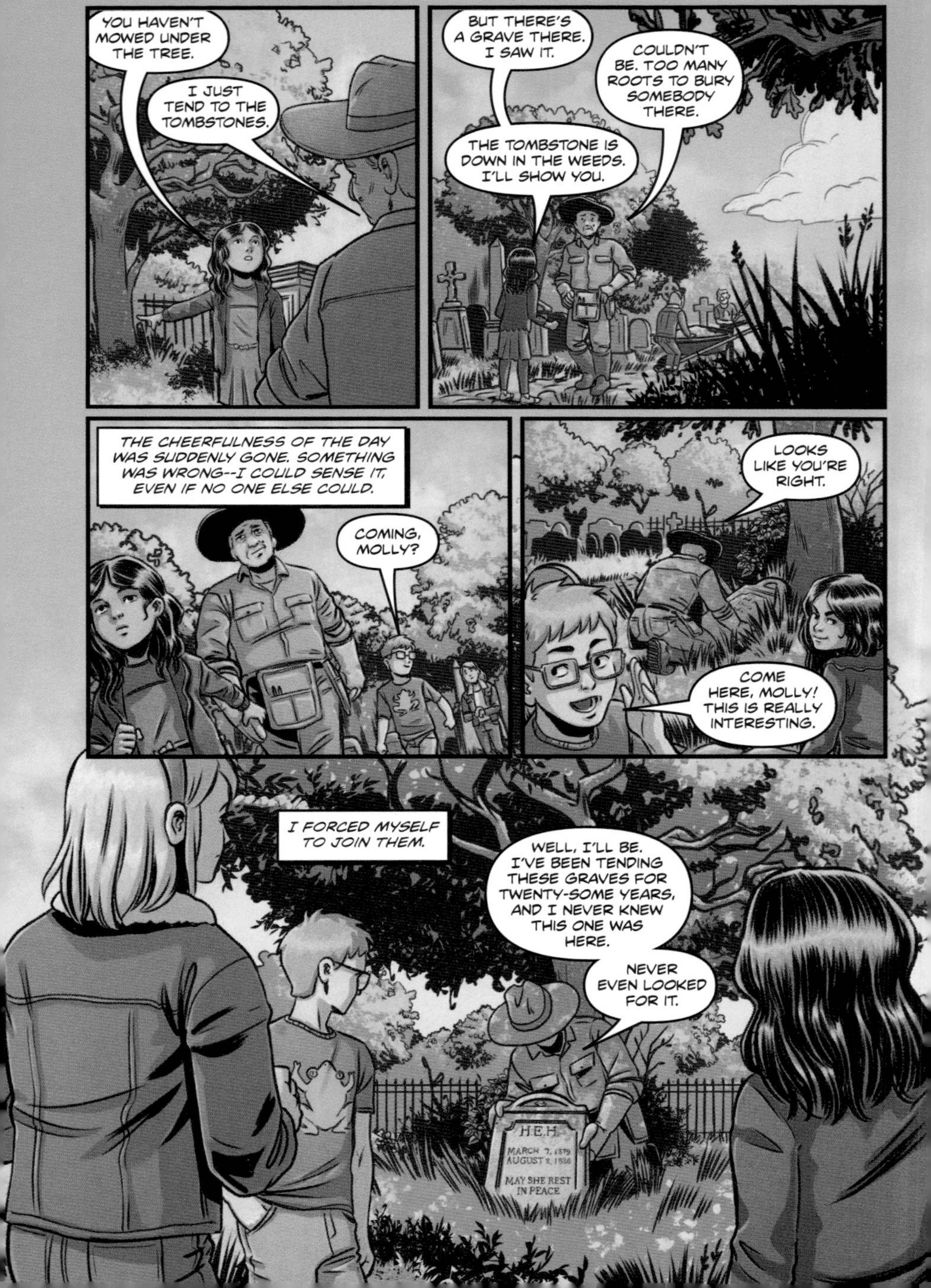
YOU HAVEN'T MOWED UNDER THE TREE.
I JUST TEND TO THE TOMBSTONES.
BUT THERE'S A GRAVE THERE. I SAW IT.
COULDN'T BE. TOO MANY ROOTS TO BURY SOMEBODY THERE.
THE TOMBSTONE IS DOWN IN THE WEEDS. I'LL SHOW YOU.
THE CHEERFULNESS OF THE DAY WAS SUDDENLY GONE. SOMETHING WAS WRONG--I COULD SENSE IT, EVEN IF NO ONE ELSE COULD.
COMING, MOLLY?
LOOKS LIKE YOU'RE RIGHT.
COME HERE, MOLLY! THIS IS REALLY INTERESTING.
I FORCED MYSELF TO JOIN THEM.
WELL, I'LL BE. I'VE BEEN TENDING THESE GRAVES FOR TWENTY-SOME YEARS, AND I NEVER KNEW THIS ONE WAS HERE.
NEVER EVEN LOOKED FOR IT.
H.E.H.
MARCH 7, 1879
AUGUST 8, 1886
MAY SHE REST IN PEACE

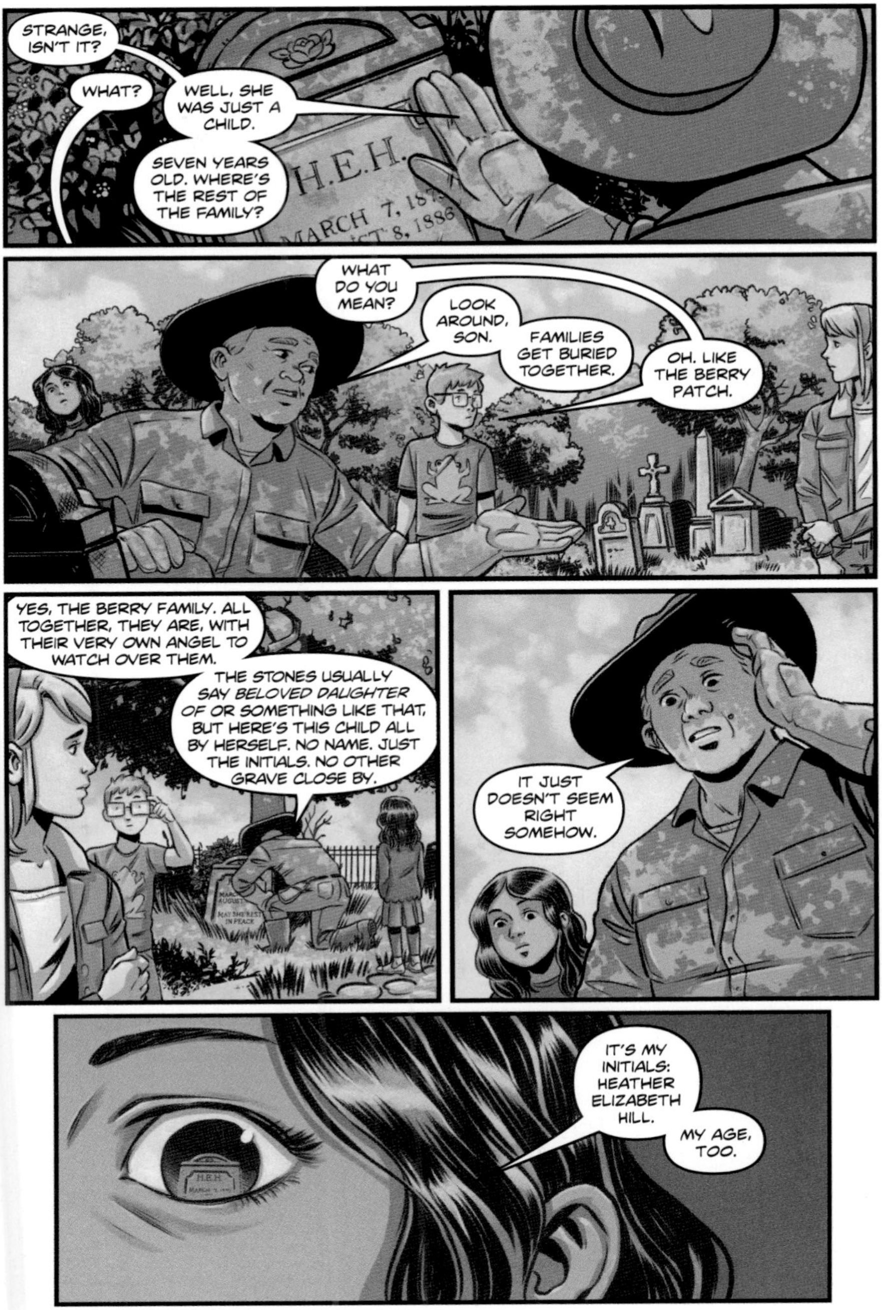
STRANGE, ISN'T IT?
WHAT?
WELL, SHE WAS JUST A CHILD.
SEVEN YEARS OLD. WHERE'S THE REST OF THE FAMILY?
H.E.H.
WHAT DO YOU MEAN?
LOOK AROUND, SON.
FAMILIES GET BURIED TOGETHER.
OH. LIKE THE BERRY PATCH.
YES, THE BERRY FAMILY. ALL TOGETHER, THEY ARE, WITH THEIR VERY OWN ANGEL TO WATCH OVER THEM.
THE STONES USUALLY SAY *BELOVED DAUGHTER OF* OR SOMETHING LIKE THAT, BUT HERE'S THIS CHILD ALL BY HERSELF. NO NAME. JUST THE INITIALS. NO OTHER GRAVE CLOSE BY.
MAY SHE REST IN PEACE
IT JUST DOESN'T SEEM RIGHT SOMEHOW.
IT'S MY INITIALS: HEATHER ELIZABETH HILL.
MY AGE, TOO.

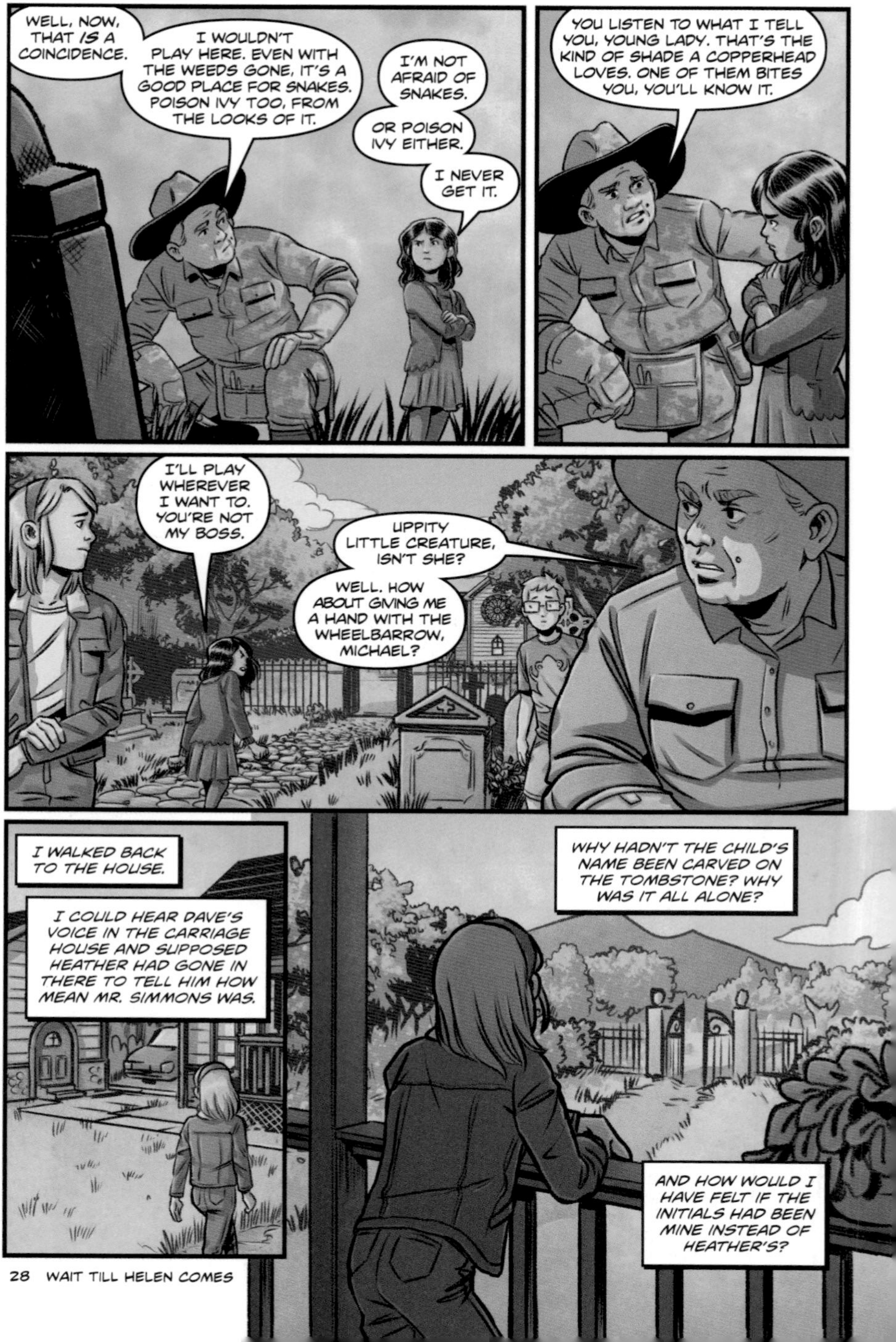
WELL, NOW, THAT *IS* A COINCIDENCE.
I WOULDN'T PLAY HERE. EVEN WITH THE WEEDS GONE, IT'S A GOOD PLACE FOR SNAKES. POISON IVY TOO, FROM THE LOOKS OF IT.
I'M NOT AFRAID OF SNAKES.
OR POISON IVY EITHER.
I NEVER GET IT.
YOU LISTEN TO WHAT I TELL YOU, YOUNG LADY. THAT'S THE KIND OF SHADE A COPPERHEAD LOVES. ONE OF THEM BITES YOU, YOU'LL KNOW IT.
I'LL PLAY WHEREVER I WANT TO. YOU'RE NOT MY BOSS.
UPPITY LITTLE CREATURE, ISN'T SHE?
WELL. HOW ABOUT GIVING ME A HAND WITH THE WHEELBARROW, MICHAEL?
I WALKED BACK TO THE HOUSE.
I COULD HEAR DAVE'S VOICE IN THE CARRIAGE HOUSE AND SUPPOSED HEATHER HAD GONE IN THERE TO TELL HIM HOW MEAN MR. SIMMONS WAS.
WHY HADN'T THE CHILD'S NAME BEEN CARVED ON THE TOMBSTONE? WHY WAS IT ALL ALONE?
AND HOW WOULD I HAVE FELT IF THE INITIALS HAD BEEN MINE INSTEAD OF HEATHER'S?

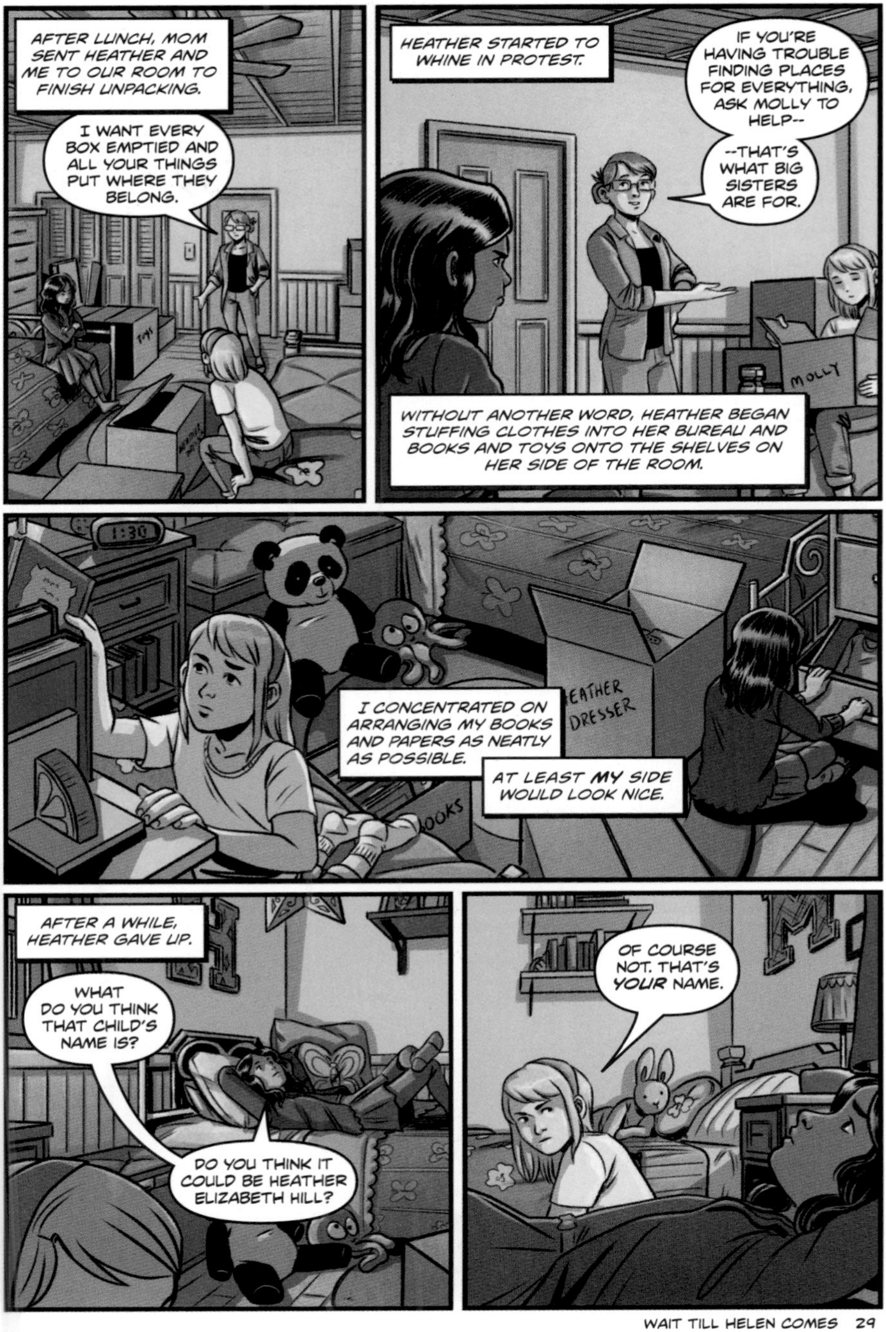
AFTER LUNCH, MOM SENT HEATHER AND ME TO OUR ROOM TO FINISH UNPACKING.
I WANT EVERY BOX EMPTIED AND ALL YOUR THINGS PUT WHERE THEY BELONG.
TOYS
HEATHER STARTED TO WHINE IN PROTEST.
IF YOU'RE HAVING TROUBLE FINDING PLACES FOR EVERYTHING, ASK MOLLY TO HELP--
--THAT'S WHAT BIG SISTERS ARE FOR.
MOLLY
WITHOUT ANOTHER WORD, HEATHER BEGAN STUFFING CLOTHES INTO HER BUREAU AND BOOKS AND TOYS ONTO THE SHELVES ON HER SIDE OF THE ROOM.
1:30
HEATHER DRESSER
I CONCENTRATED ON ARRANGING MY BOOKS AND PAPERS AS NEATLY AS POSSIBLE.
AT LEAST MY SIDE WOULD LOOK NICE.
BOOKS
AFTER A WHILE, HEATHER GAVE UP.
WHAT DO YOU THINK THAT CHILD'S NAME IS?
DO YOU THINK IT COULD BE HEATHER ELIZABETH HILL?
OF COURSE NOT. THAT'S *YOUR* NAME.

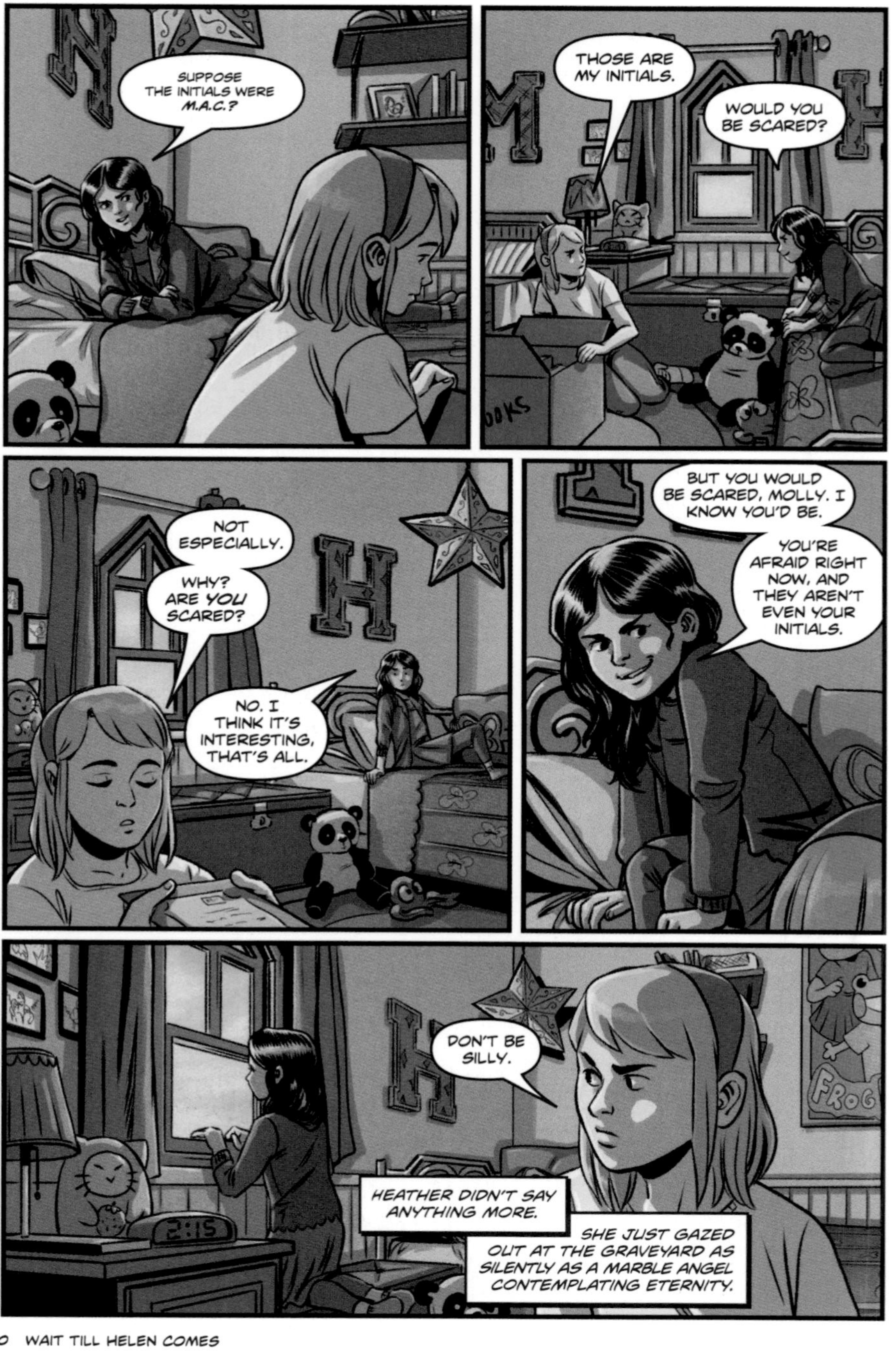
SUPPOSE THE INITIALS WERE *M.A.C.?*
THOSE ARE MY INITIALS.
WOULD YOU BE SCARED?
OOKS
NOT ESPECIALLY.
WHY? ARE *YOU* SCARED?
NO. I THINK IT'S INTERESTING, THAT'S ALL.
BUT YOU WOULD BE SCARED, MOLLY. I KNOW YOU'D BE.
YOU'RE AFRAID RIGHT NOW, AND THEY AREN'T EVEN YOUR INITIALS.
DON'T BE SILLY.
2:15
FROG
HEATHER DIDN'T SAY ANYTHING MORE.
SHE JUST GAZED OUT AT THE GRAVEYARD AS SILENTLY AS A MARBLE ANGEL CONTEMPLATING ETERNITY.

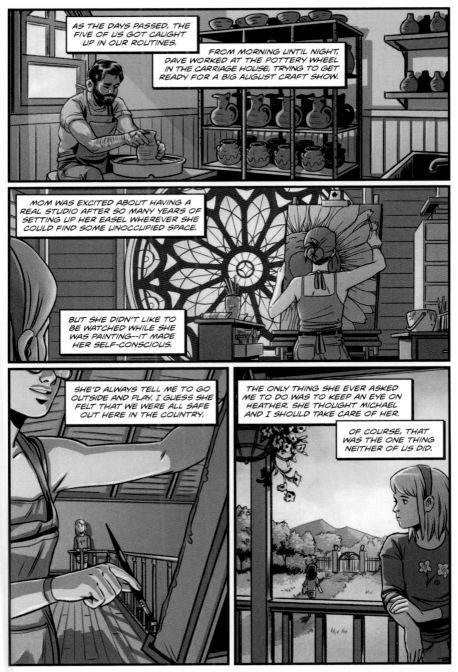

AS THE DAYS PASSED, THE FIVE OF US GOT CAUGHT UP IN OUR ROUTINES.

FROM MORNING UNTIL NIGHT, DAVE WORKED AT THE POTTERY WHEEL IN THE CARRIAGE HOUSE, TRYING TO GET READY FOR A BIG AUGUST CRAFT SHOW.

MOM WAS EXCITED ABOUT HAVING A REAL STUDIO AFTER SO MANY YEARS OF SETTING UP HER EASEL WHEREVER SHE COULD FIND SOME UNOCCUPIED SPACE.

BUT SHE DIDN'T LIKE TO BE WATCHED WHILE SHE WAS PAINTING--IT MADE HER SELF-CONSCIOUS.

SHE'D ALWAYS TELL ME TO GO OUTSIDE AND PLAY. I GUESS SHE FELT THAT WE WERE ALL SAFE OUT HERE IN THE COUNTRY.

THE ONLY THING SHE EVER ASKED ME TO DO WAS TO KEEP AN EYE ON HEATHER. SHE THOUGHT MICHAEL AND I SHOULD TAKE CARE OF HER.

OF COURSE, THAT WAS THE ONE THING NEITHER OF US DID.

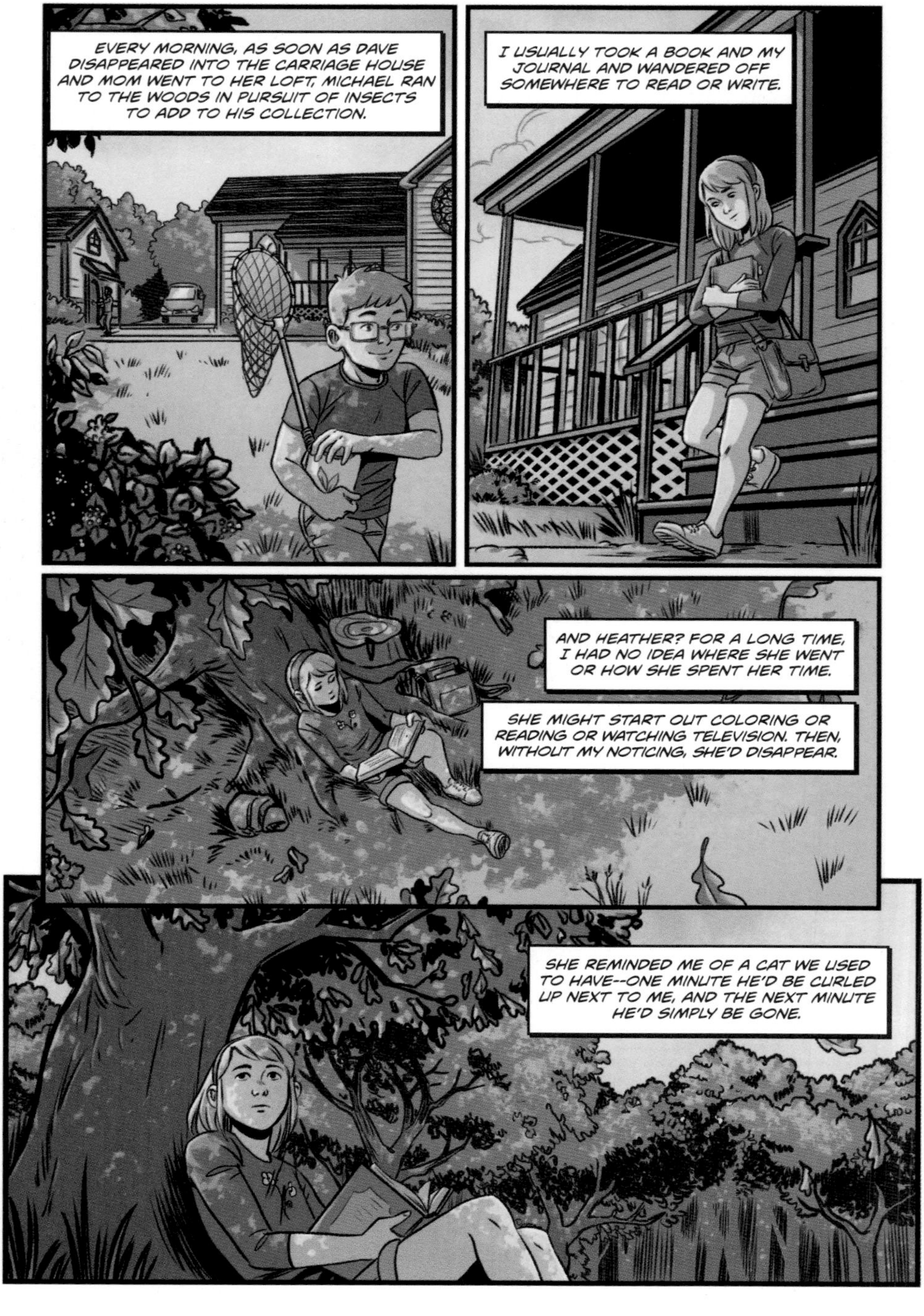
EVERY MORNING, AS SOON AS DAVE DISAPPEARED INTO THE CARRIAGE HOUSE AND MOM WENT TO HER LOFT, MICHAEL RAN TO THE WOODS IN PURSUIT OF INSECTS TO ADD TO HIS COLLECTION.
I USUALLY TOOK A BOOK AND MY JOURNAL AND WANDERED OFF SOMEWHERE TO READ OR WRITE.
AND HEATHER? FOR A LONG TIME, I HAD NO IDEA WHERE SHE WENT OR HOW SHE SPENT HER TIME.
SHE MIGHT START OUT COLORING OR READING OR WATCHING TELEVISION. THEN, WITHOUT MY NOTICING, SHE'D DISAPPEAR.
SHE REMINDED ME OF A CAT WE USED TO HAVE--ONE MINUTE HE'D BE CURLED UP NEXT TO ME, AND THE NEXT MINUTE HE'D SIMPLY BE GONE.

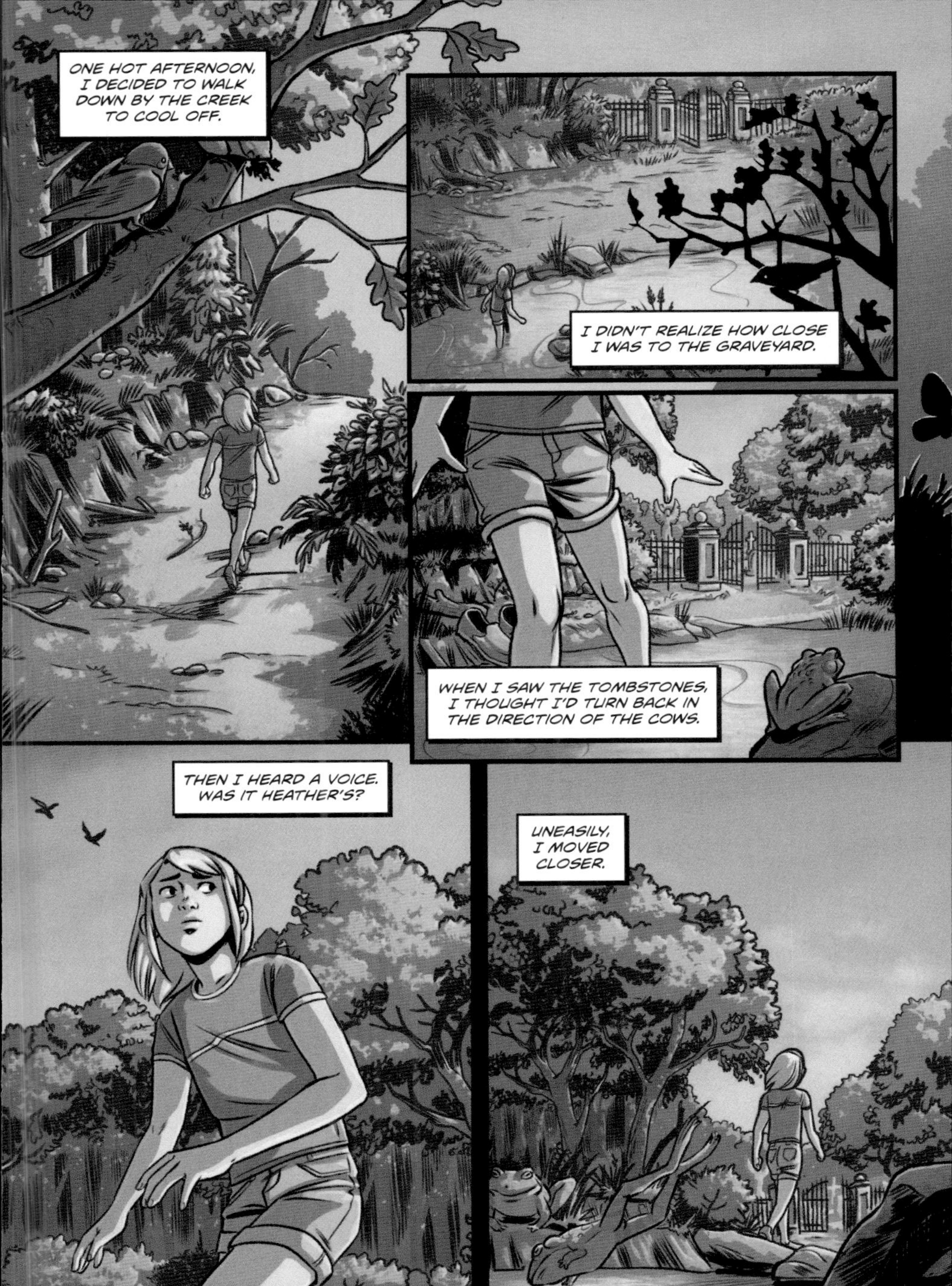
ONE HOT AFTERNOON, I DECIDED TO WALK DOWN BY THE CREEK TO COOL OFF.
I DIDN'T REALIZE HOW CLOSE I WAS TO THE GRAVEYARD.
WHEN I SAW THE TOMBSTONES, I THOUGHT I'D TURN BACK IN THE DIRECTION OF THE COWS.
THEN I HEARD A VOICE. WAS IT HEATHER'S?
UNEASILY, I MOVED CLOSER.

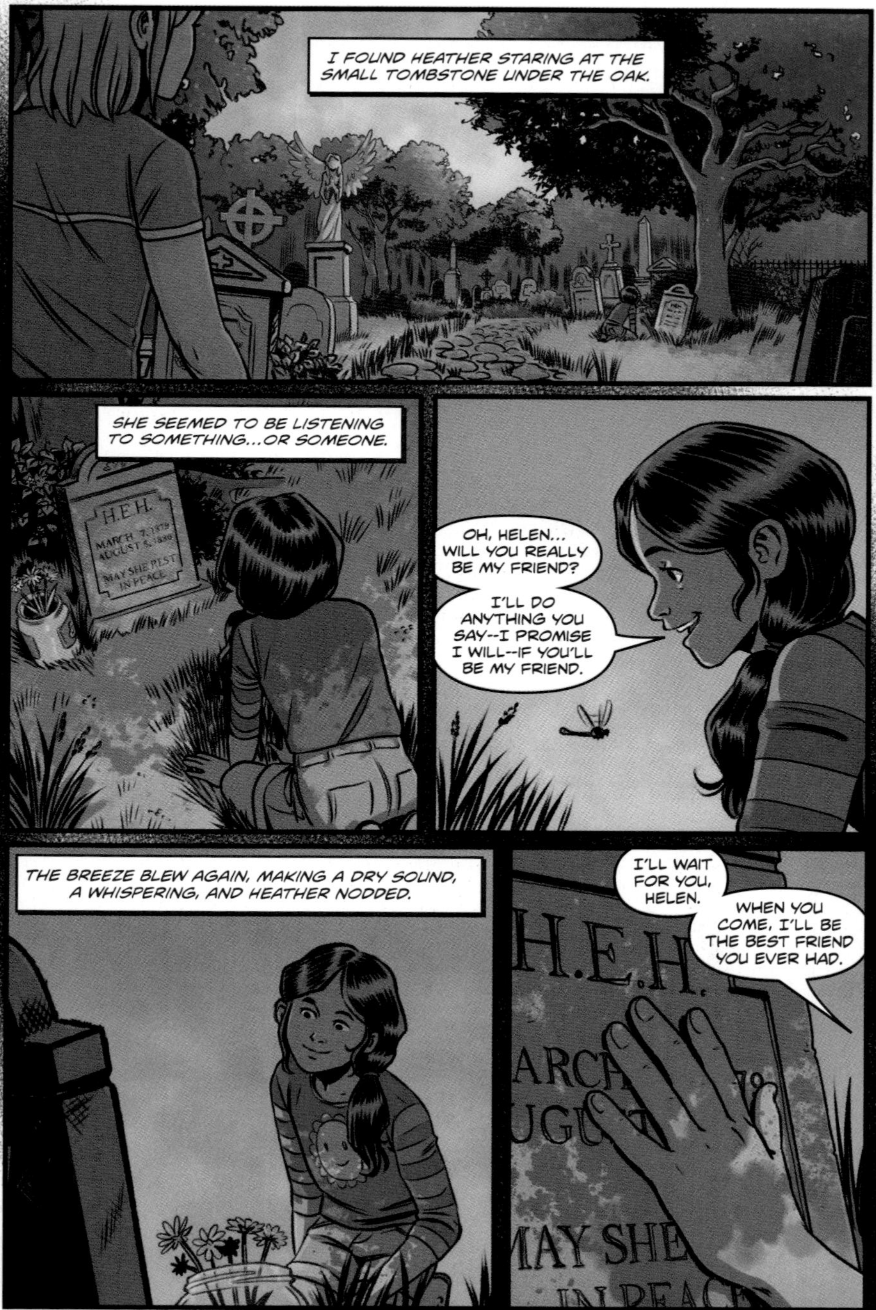
I FOUND HEATHER STARING AT THE SMALL TOMBSTONE UNDER THE OAK.
SHE SEEMED TO BE LISTENING TO SOMETHING...OR SOMEONE.
H.E.H.
MAY SHE REST IN PEACE
OH, HELEN... WILL YOU REALLY BE MY FRIEND?
I'LL DO ANYTHING YOU SAY--I PROMISE I WILL--IF YOU'LL BE MY FRIEND.
THE BREEZE BLEW AGAIN, MAKING A DRY SOUND, A WHISPERING, AND HEATHER NODDED.
I'LL WAIT FOR YOU, HELEN.
WHEN YOU COME, I'LL BE THE BEST FRIEND YOU EVER HAD.

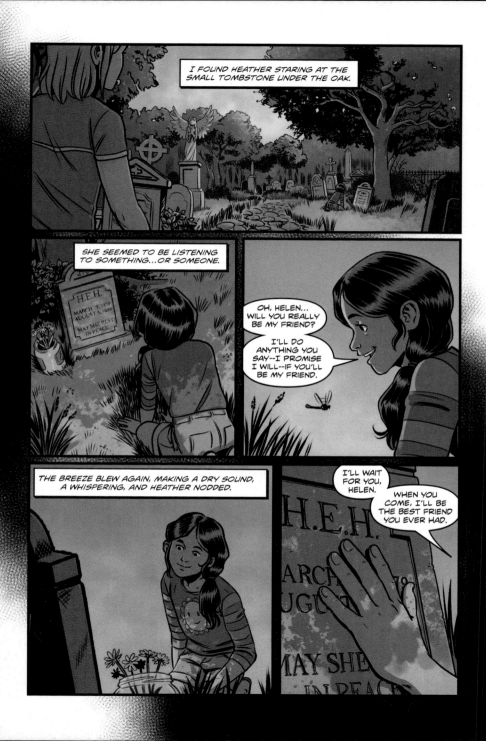

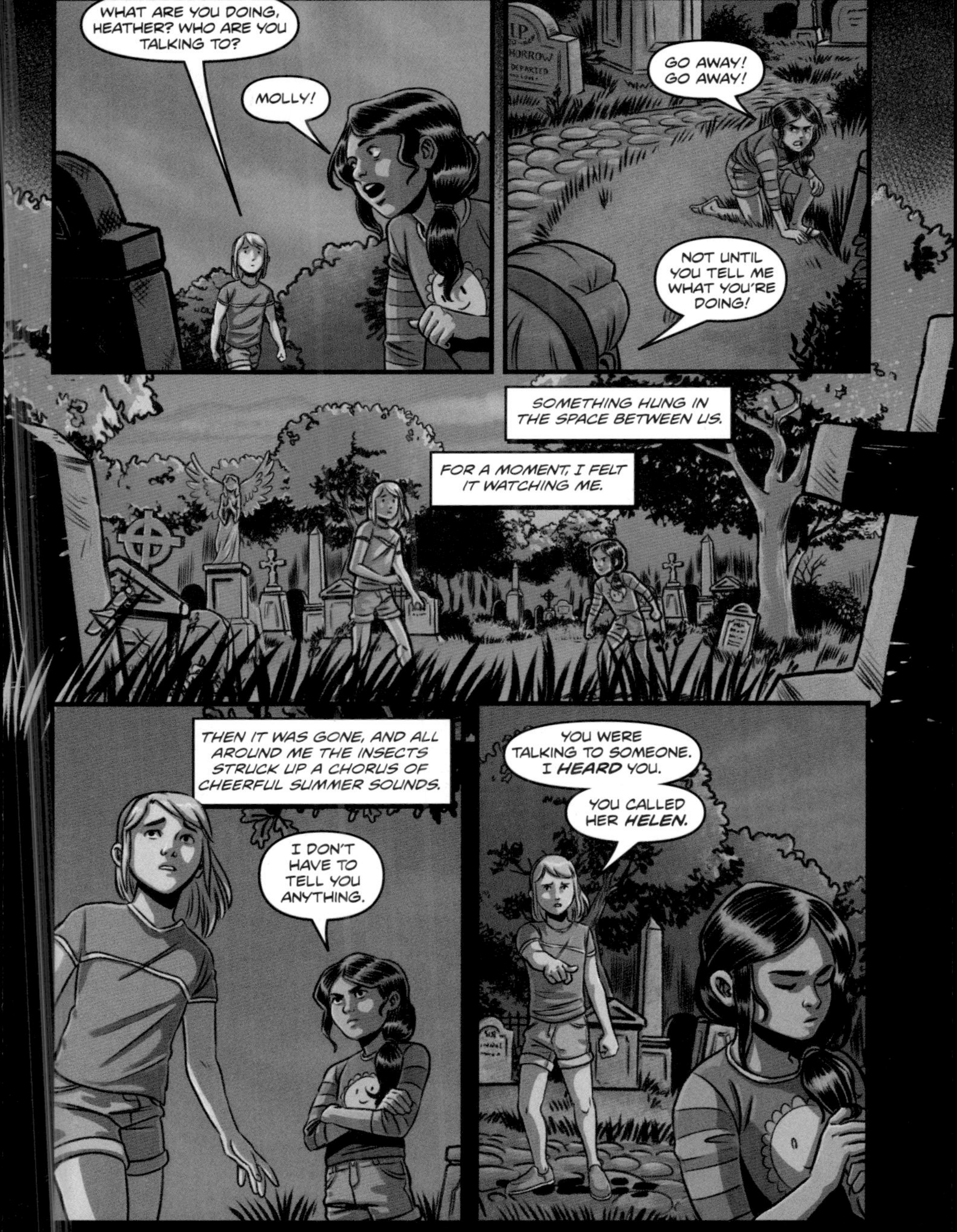
WHAT ARE YOU DOING, HEATHER? WHO ARE YOU TALKING TO?
MOLLY!
GO AWAY! GO AWAY!
NOT UNTIL YOU TELL ME WHAT YOU'RE DOING!
SOMETHING HUNG IN THE SPACE BETWEEN US.
FOR A MOMENT, I FELT IT WATCHING ME.
THEN IT WAS GONE, AND ALL AROUND ME THE INSECTS STRUCK UP A CHORUS OF CHEERFUL SUMMER SOUNDS.
I DON'T HAVE TO TELL YOU ANYTHING.
YOU WERE TALKING TO SOMEONE. I HEARD YOU.
YOU CALLED HER HELEN.

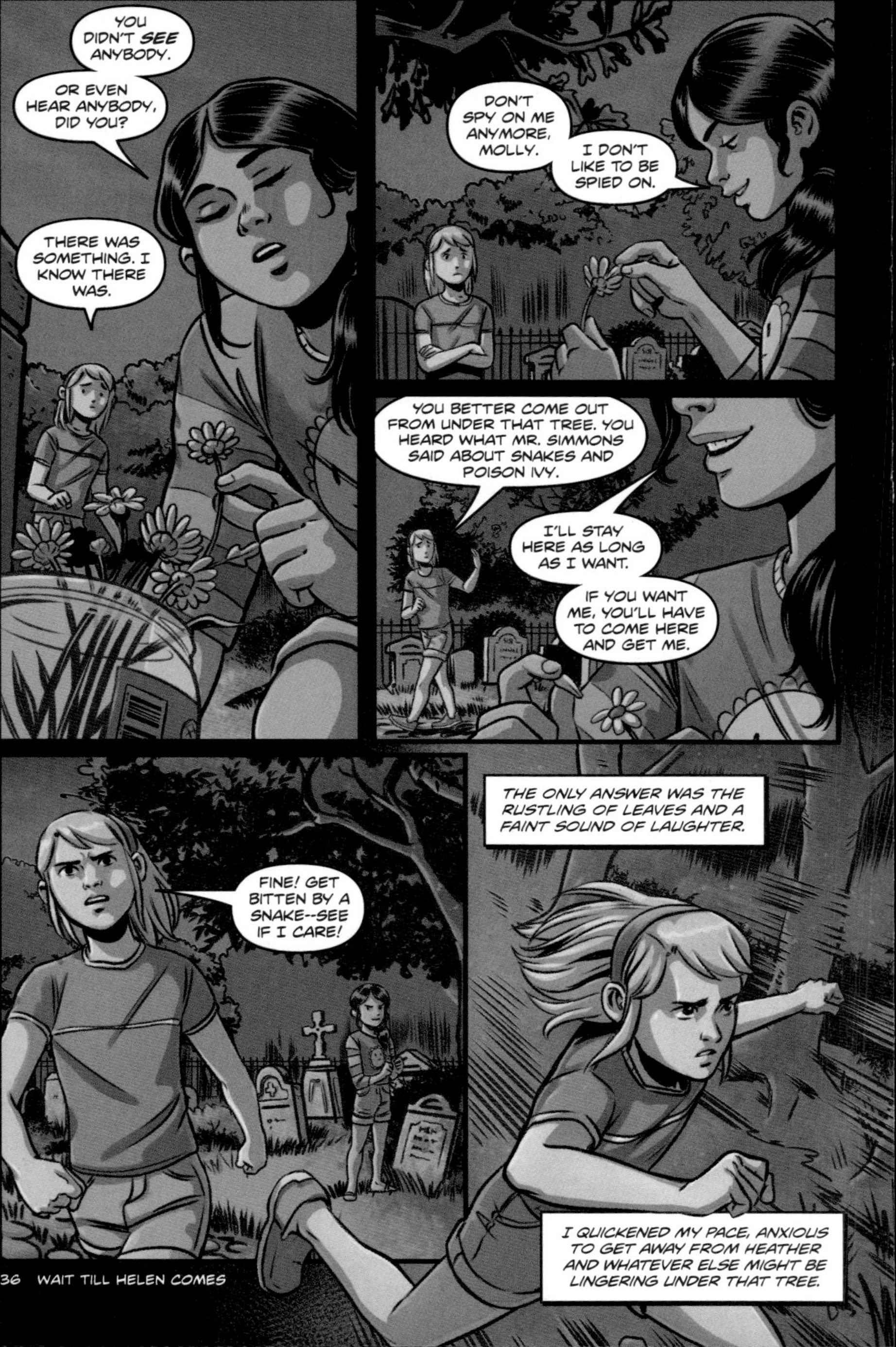
YOU DIDN'T *SEE* ANYBODY.
OR EVEN HEAR ANYBODY, DID YOU?
THERE WAS SOMETHING. I KNOW THERE WAS.
DON'T SPY ON ME ANYMORE, MOLLY.
I DON'T LIKE TO BE SPIED ON.
YOU BETTER COME OUT FROM UNDER THAT TREE. YOU HEARD WHAT MR. SIMMONS SAID ABOUT SNAKES AND POISON IVY.
I'LL STAY HERE AS LONG AS I WANT.
IF YOU WANT ME, YOU'LL HAVE TO COME HERE AND GET ME.
FINE! GET BITTEN BY A SNAKE--SEE IF I CARE!
THE ONLY ANSWER WAS THE RUSTLING OF LEAVES AND A FAINT SOUND OF LAUGHTER.
I QUICKENED MY PACE, ANXIOUS TO GET AWAY FROM HEATHER AND WHATEVER ELSE MIGHT BE LINGERING UNDER THAT TREE.

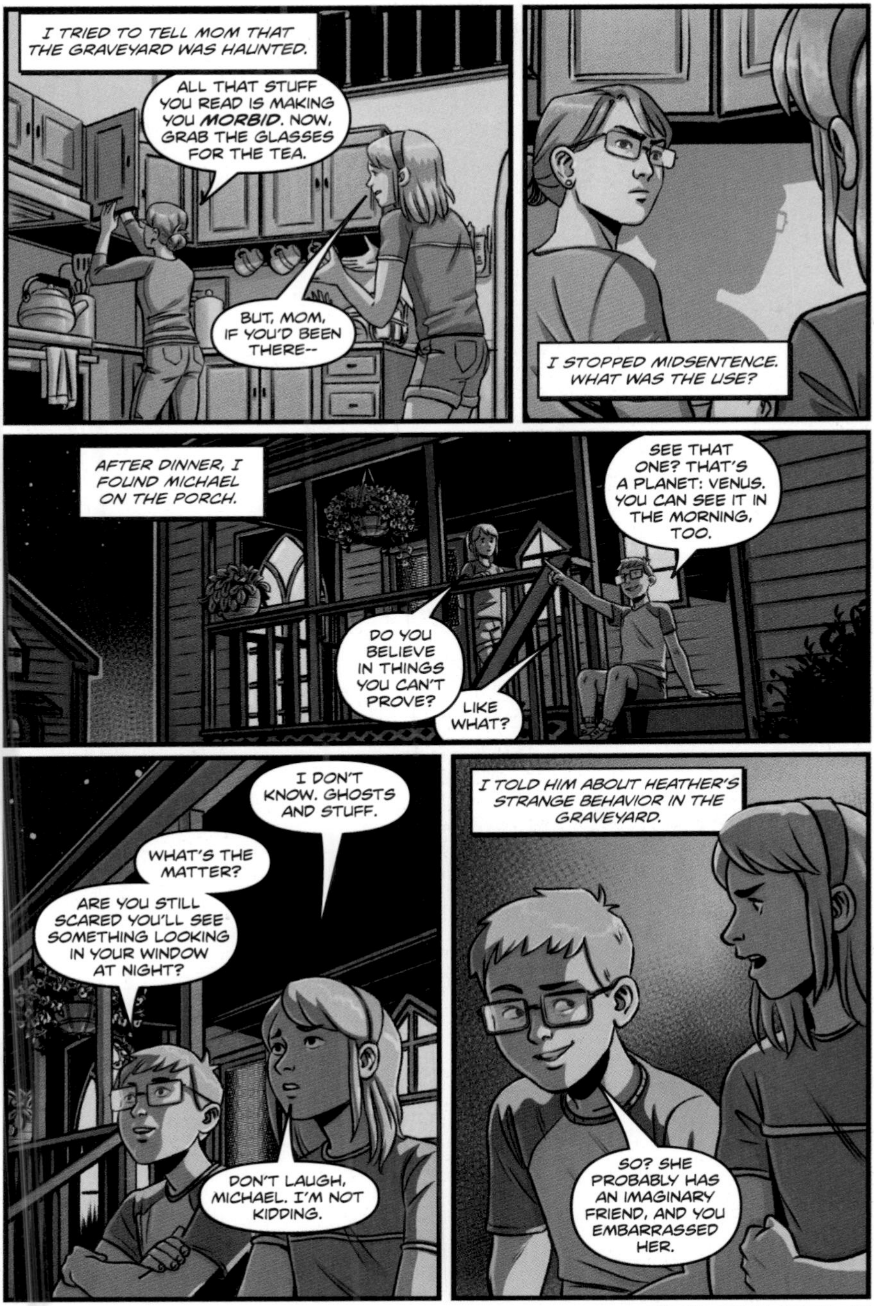
I TRIED TO TELL MOM THAT THE GRAVEYARD WAS HAUNTED.
ALL THAT STUFF YOU READ IS MAKING YOU **MORBID**. NOW, GRAB THE GLASSES FOR THE TEA.
BUT, MOM, IF YOU'D BEEN THERE--
I STOPPED MIDSENTENCE. WHAT WAS THE USE?
AFTER DINNER, I FOUND MICHAEL ON THE PORCH.
SEE THAT ONE? THAT'S A PLANET: VENUS. YOU CAN SEE IT IN THE MORNING, TOO.
DO YOU BELIEVE IN THINGS YOU CAN'T PROVE?
LIKE WHAT?
I DON'T KNOW. GHOSTS AND STUFF.
WHAT'S THE MATTER?
ARE YOU STILL SCARED YOU'LL SEE SOMETHING LOOKING IN YOUR WINDOW AT NIGHT?
DON'T LAUGH, MICHAEL. I'M NOT KIDDING.
I TOLD HIM ABOUT HEATHER'S STRANGE BEHAVIOR IN THE GRAVEYARD.
SO? SHE PROBABLY HAS AN IMAGINARY FRIEND, AND YOU EMBARRASSED HER.

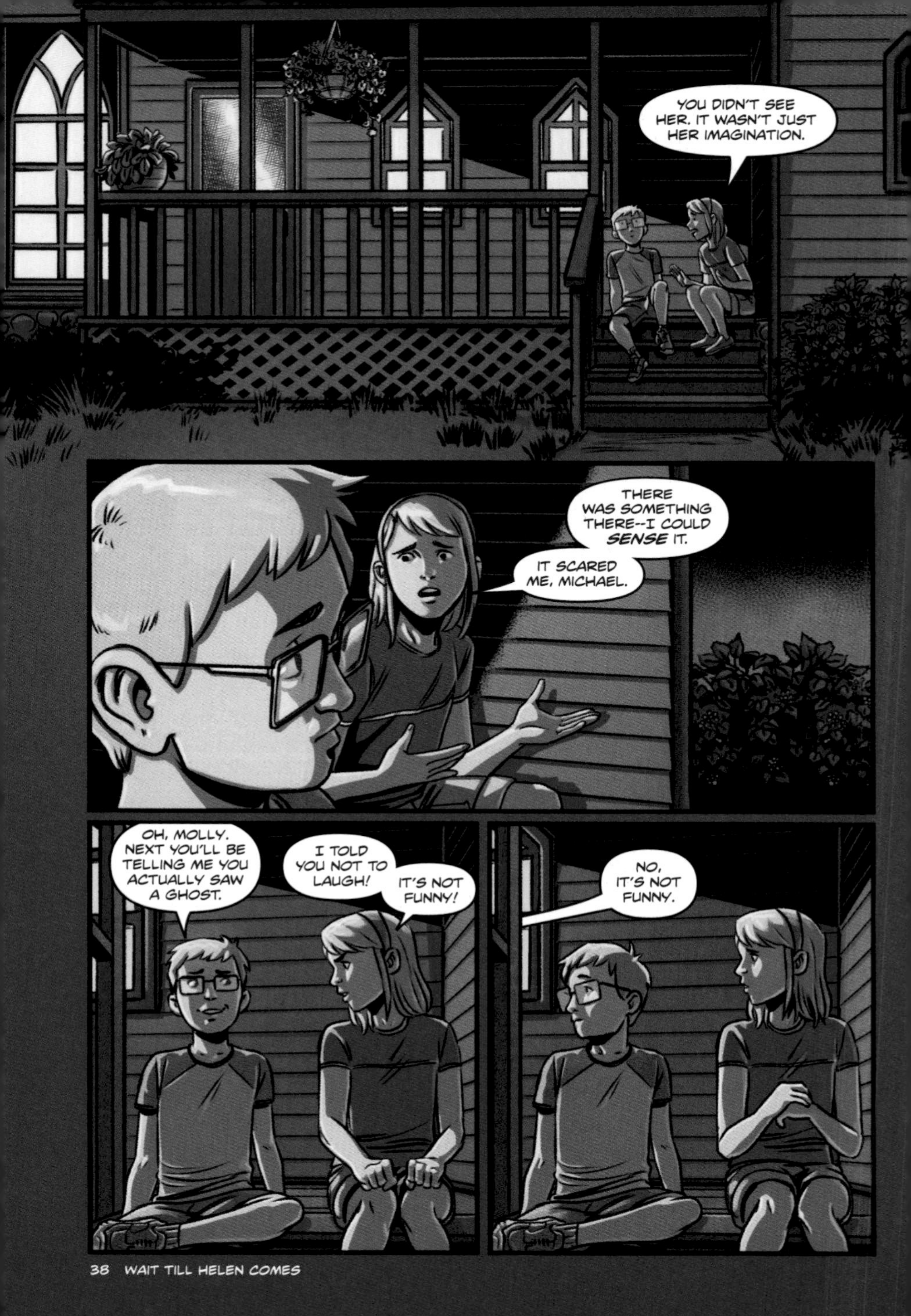
YOU DIDN'T SEE HER. IT WASN'T JUST HER IMAGINATION.
THERE WAS SOMETHING THERE--I COULD *SENSE* IT.
IT SCARED ME, MICHAEL.
OH, MOLLY. NEXT YOU'LL BE TELLING ME YOU ACTUALLY SAW A GHOST.
I TOLD YOU NOT TO LAUGH!
IT'S NOT FUNNY!
NO, IT'S NOT FUNNY.

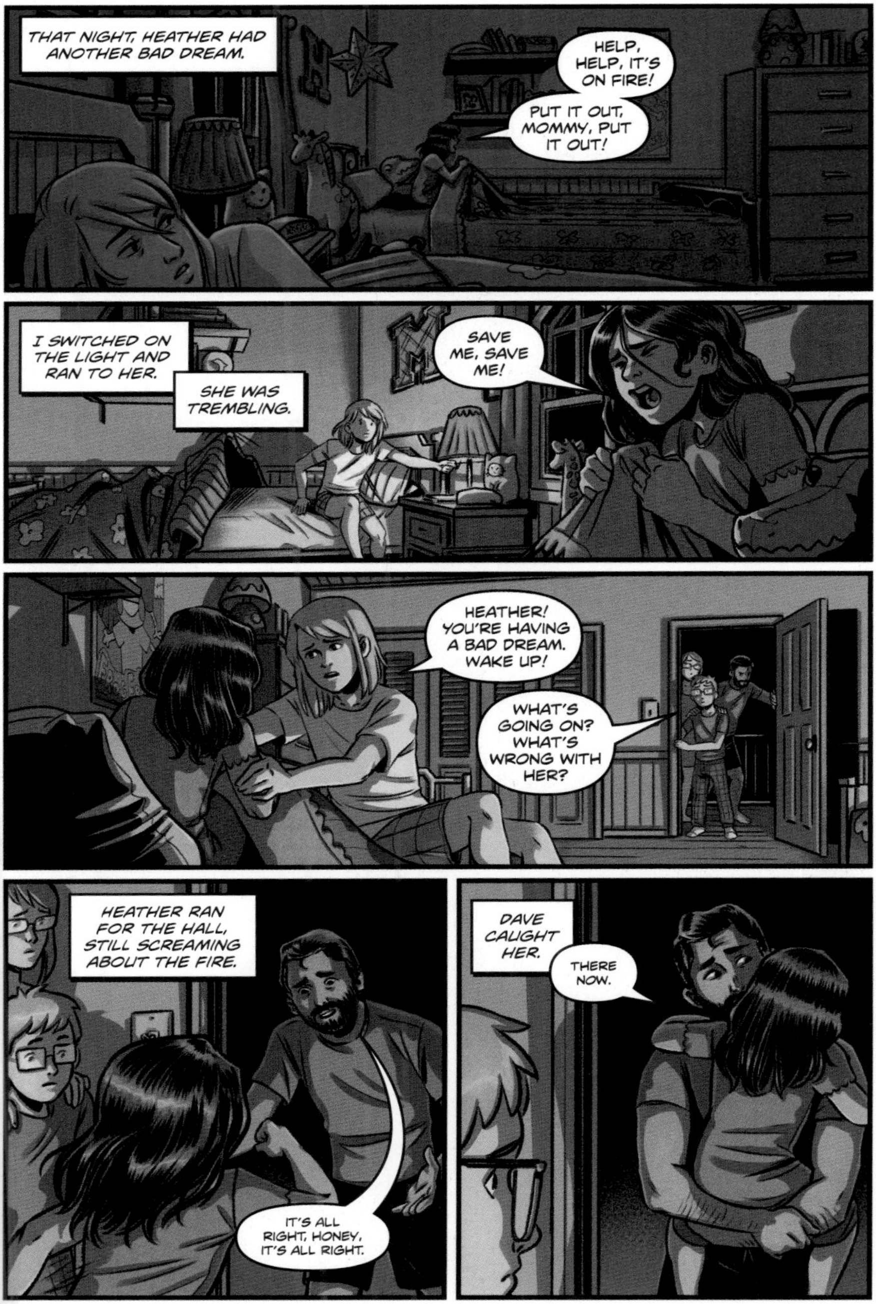
THAT NIGHT, HEATHER HAD ANOTHER BAD DREAM.
HELP, HELP, IT'S ON FIRE!
PUT IT OUT, MOMMY, PUT IT OUT!
I SWITCHED ON THE LIGHT AND RAN TO HER.
SHE WAS TREMBLING.
SAVE ME, SAVE ME!
HEATHER! YOU'RE HAVING A BAD DREAM. WAKE UP!
WHAT'S GOING ON? WHAT'S WRONG WITH HER?
HEATHER RAN FOR THE HALL, STILL SCREAMING ABOUT THE FIRE.
IT'S ALL RIGHT, HONEY, IT'S ALL RIGHT.
DAVE CAUGHT HER.
THERE NOW.

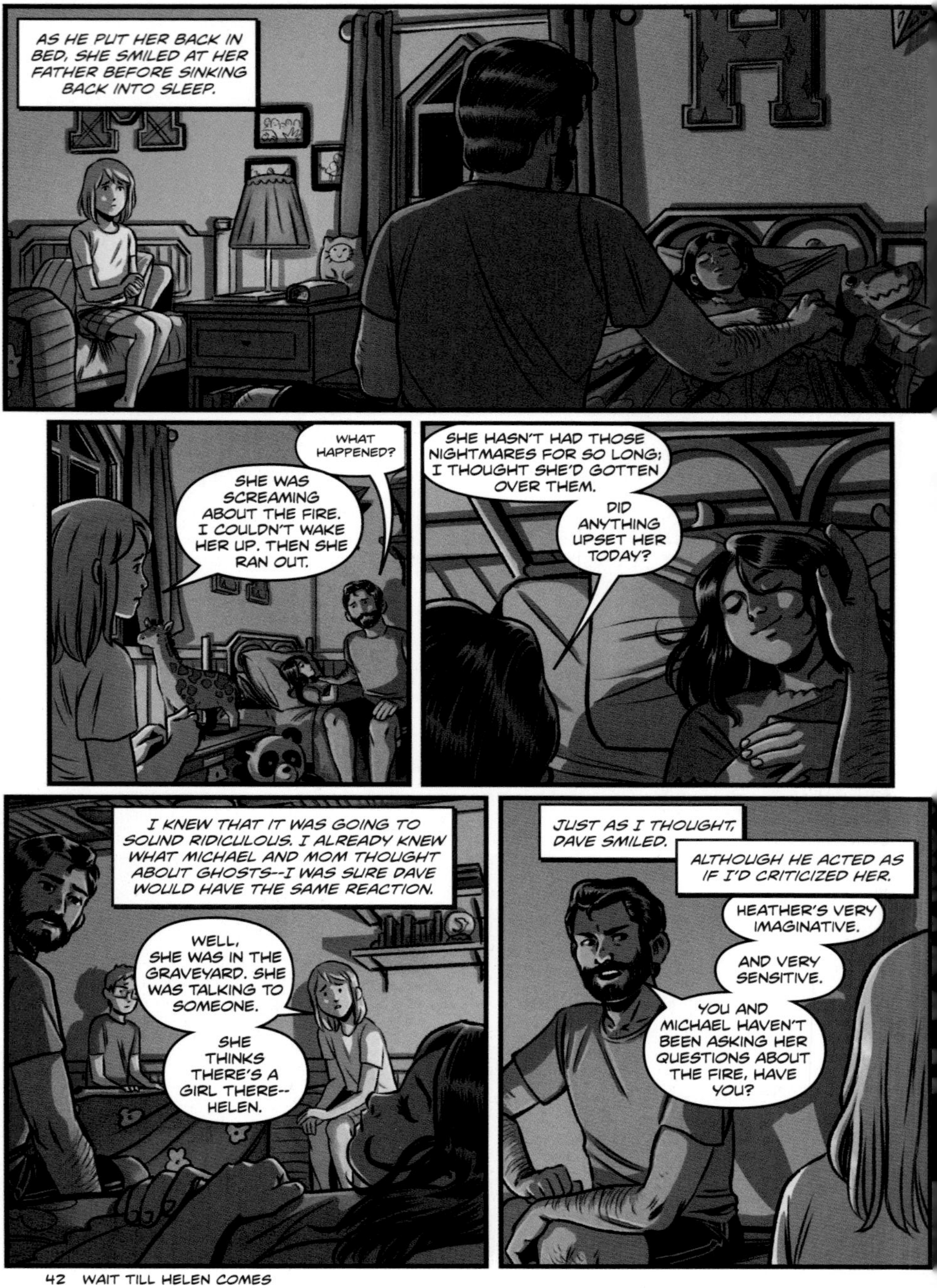
AS HE PUT HER BACK IN BED, SHE SMILED AT HER FATHER BEFORE SINKING BACK INTO SLEEP.
WHAT HAPPENED?
SHE WAS SCREAMING ABOUT THE FIRE. I COULDN'T WAKE HER UP. THEN SHE RAN OUT.
SHE HASN'T HAD THOSE NIGHTMARES FOR SO LONG; I THOUGHT SHE'D GOTTEN OVER THEM.
DID ANYTHING UPSET HER TODAY?
I KNEW THAT IT WAS GOING TO SOUND RIDICULOUS. I ALREADY KNEW WHAT MICHAEL AND MOM THOUGHT ABOUT GHOSTS--I WAS SURE DAVE WOULD HAVE THE SAME REACTION.
WELL, SHE WAS IN THE GRAVEYARD. SHE WAS TALKING TO SOMEONE.
SHE THINKS THERE'S A GIRL THERE--HELEN.
JUST AS I THOUGHT, DAVE SMILED.
ALTHOUGH HE ACTED AS IF I'D CRITICIZED HER.
HEATHER'S VERY IMAGINATIVE.
AND VERY SENSITIVE.
YOU AND MICHAEL HAVEN'T BEEN ASKING HER QUESTIONS ABOUT THE FIRE, HAVE YOU?

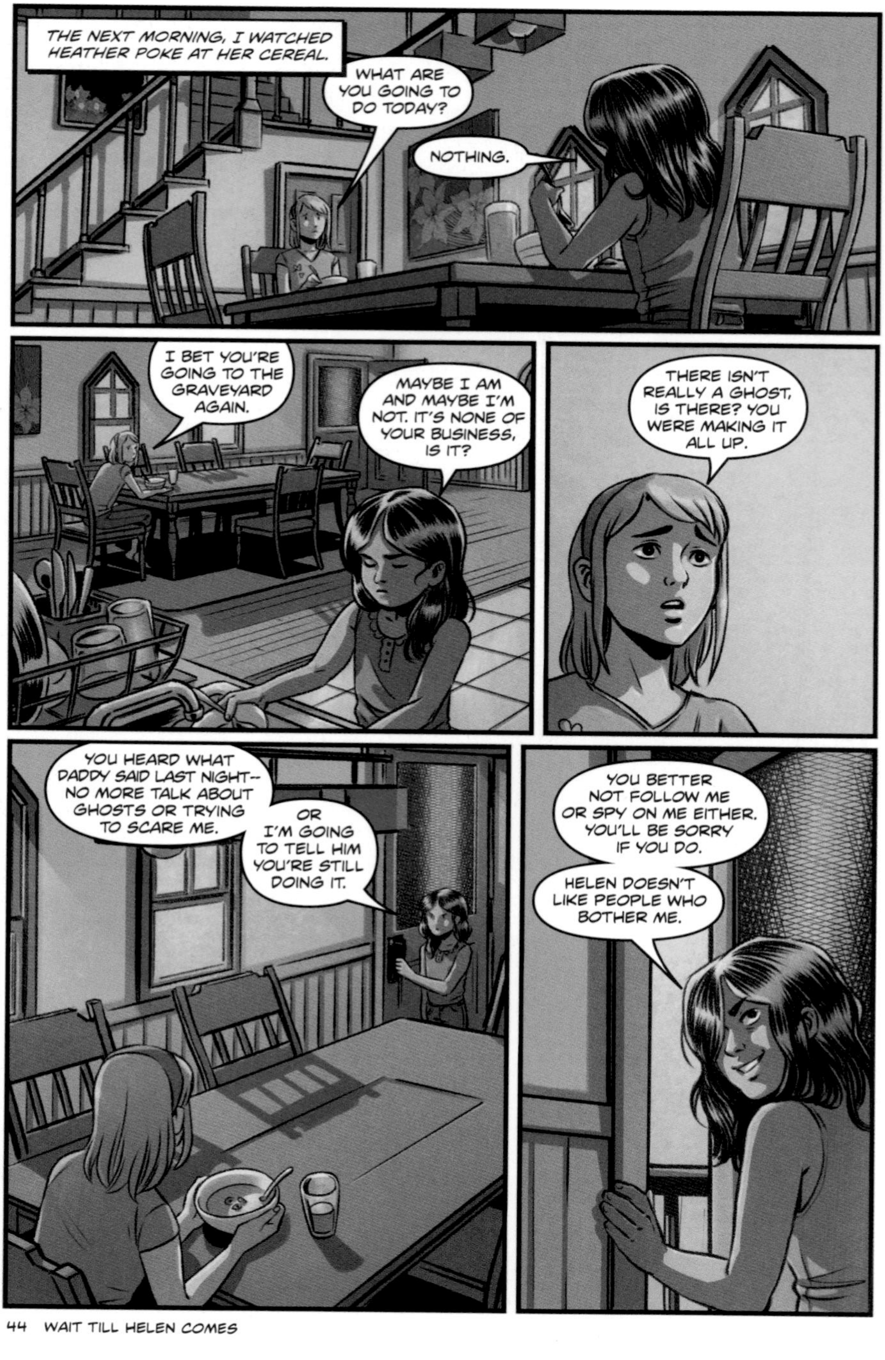
THE NEXT MORNING, I WATCHED HEATHER POKE AT HER CEREAL.
WHAT ARE YOU GOING TO DO TODAY?
NOTHING.
I BET YOU'RE GOING TO THE GRAVEYARD AGAIN.
MAYBE I AM AND MAYBE I'M NOT. IT'S NONE OF YOUR BUSINESS, IS IT?
THERE ISN'T REALLY A GHOST, IS THERE? YOU WERE MAKING IT ALL UP.
YOU HEARD WHAT DADDY SAID LAST NIGHT-- NO MORE TALK ABOUT GHOSTS OR TRYING TO SCARE ME.
OR I'M GOING TO TELL HIM YOU'RE STILL DOING IT.
YOU BETTER NOT FOLLOW ME OR SPY ON ME EITHER. YOU'LL BE SORRY IF YOU DO.
HELEN DOESN'T LIKE PEOPLE WHO BOTHER ME.

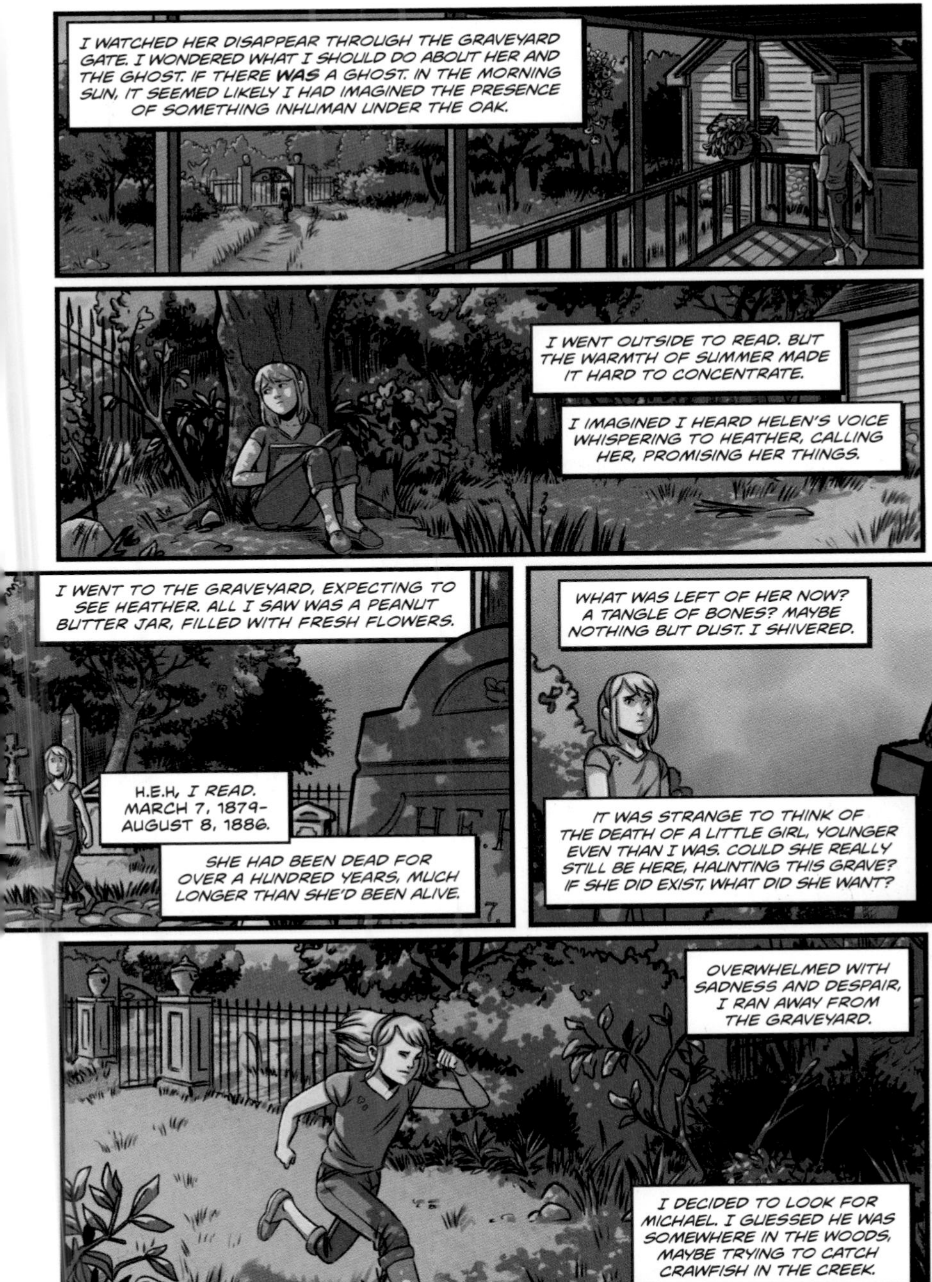
I WATCHED HER DISAPPEAR THROUGH THE GRAVEYARD GATE. I WONDERED WHAT I SHOULD DO ABOUT HER AND THE GHOST. IF THERE **WAS** A GHOST. IN THE MORNING SUN, IT SEEMED LIKELY I HAD IMAGINED THE PRESENCE OF SOMETHING INHUMAN UNDER THE OAK.
I WENT OUTSIDE TO READ. BUT THE WARMTH OF SUMMER MADE IT HARD TO CONCENTRATE.
I IMAGINED I HEARD HELEN'S VOICE WHISPERING TO HEATHER, CALLING HER, PROMISING HER THINGS.
I WENT TO THE GRAVEYARD, EXPECTING TO SEE HEATHER. ALL I SAW WAS A PEANUT BUTTER JAR, FILLED WITH FRESH FLOWERS.
H.E.H, I READ. MARCH 7, 1879-AUGUST 8, 1886.
SHE HAD BEEN DEAD FOR OVER A HUNDRED YEARS, MUCH LONGER THAN SHE'D BEEN ALIVE.
WHAT WAS LEFT OF HER NOW? A TANGLE OF BONES? MAYBE NOTHING BUT DUST. I SHIVERED.
IT WAS STRANGE TO THINK OF THE DEATH OF A LITTLE GIRL, YOUNGER EVEN THAN I WAS. COULD SHE REALLY STILL BE HERE, HAUNTING THIS GRAVE? IF SHE DID EXIST, WHAT DID SHE WANT?
OVERWHELMED WITH SADNESS AND DESPAIR, I RAN AWAY FROM THE GRAVEYARD.
I DECIDED TO LOOK FOR MICHAEL. I GUESSED HE WAS SOMEWHERE IN THE WOODS, MAYBE TRYING TO CATCH CRAWFISH IN THE CREEK.

I WAS SURE THAT HEATHER COULD SEE SOMEONE OR SOMETHING, THAT SHE COULD HEAR A VOICE SPEAKING IN THE BREEZE.

I BROKE OUT IN GOOSE BUMPS, SURE--AFRAID-- THAT AT ANY MOMENT, I'D SEE WHAT HEATHER SAW.

I WAS POSITIVE THAT IF MICHAEL OR MOM OR EVEN DAVE WERE THERE, THEY'D FEEL IT TOO.

HEATHER WAS NOT SITTING ON THAT STONE PORCH WALL ALONE TALKING TO AN IMAGINARY FRIEND.

SOMETHING WAS WITH HER, AND I WAS SURE IT WAS NO FRIEND.

--AND I HAD TO GET AWAY, TO SAVE MYSELF FROM WHATEVER WAITED HERE.

I RAN, NOT CARING WHETHER HEATHER SAW ME.

ALL OF A SUDDEN, THE HOUSE SEEMED THREATENING, MORE FRIGHTENING THAN THE GRAVEYARD.

SOMETHING TERRIBLE HAD HAPPENED HERE-- I KNEW IT HAD--

ONCE I REACHED THE SAFETY OF THE WOODS, I COLLAPSED, GASPING FOR BREATH.

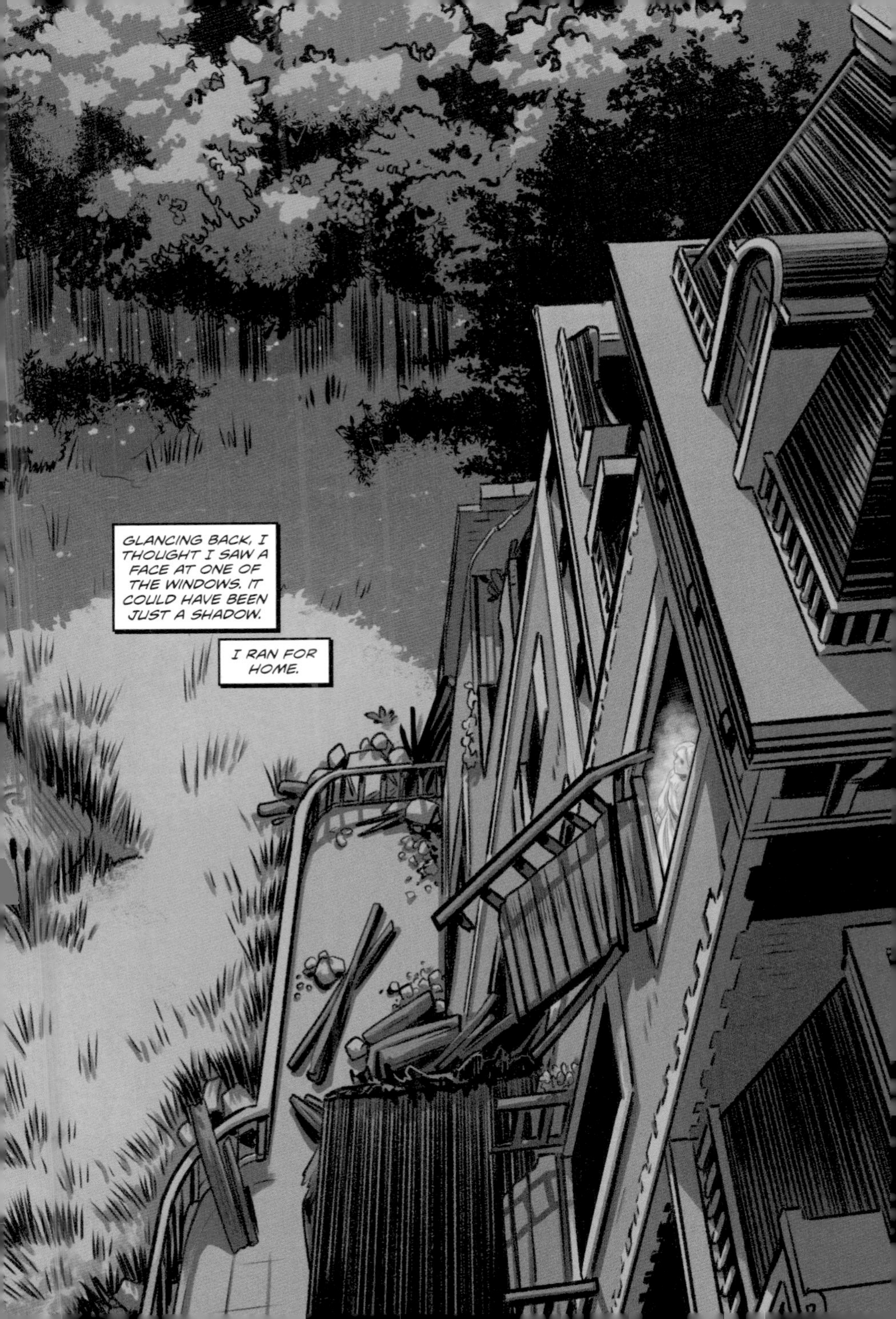
GLANCING BACK, I THOUGHT I SAW A FACE AT ONE OF THE WINDOWS. IT COULD HAVE BEEN JUST A SHADOW.
I RAN FOR HOME.

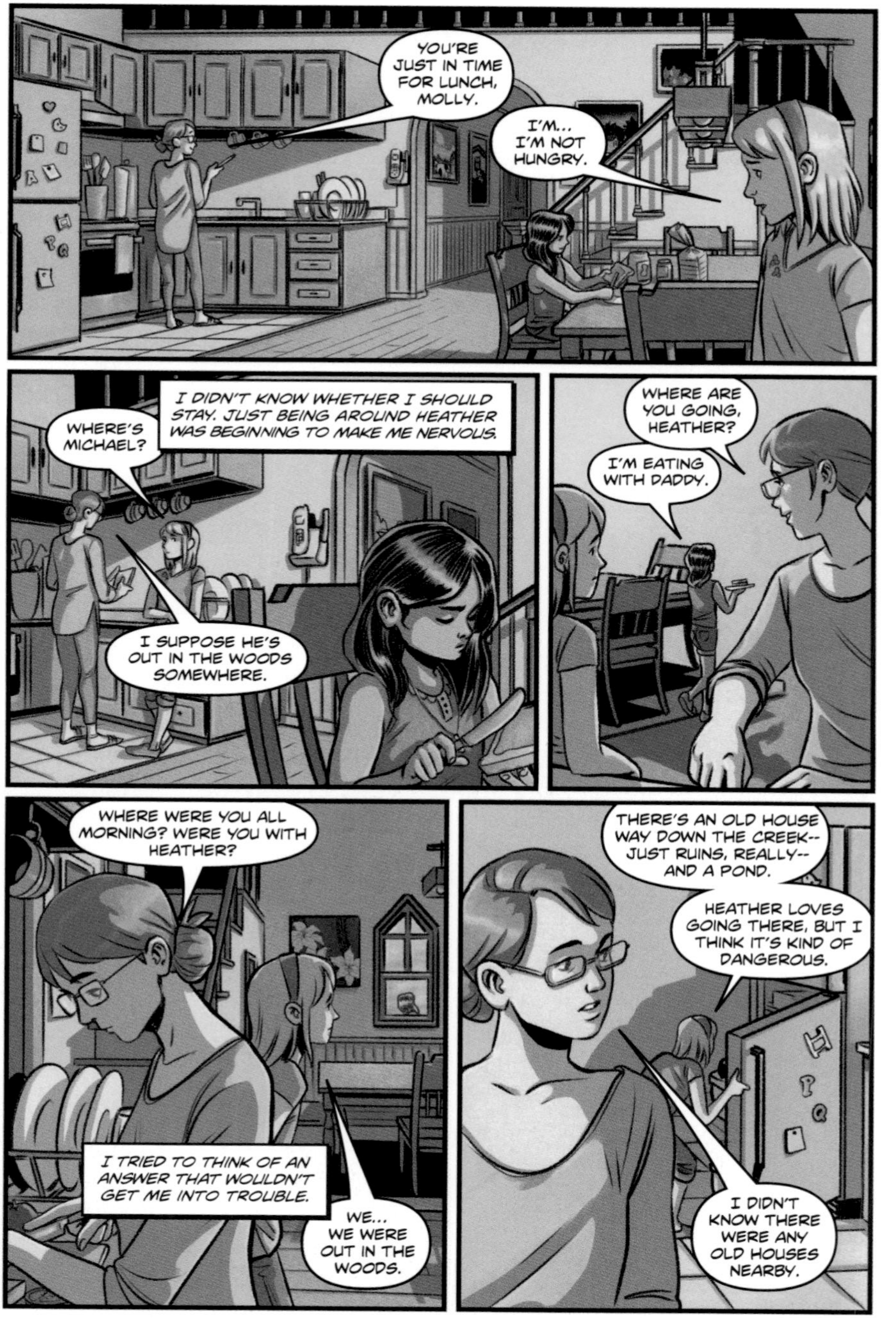
YOU'RE JUST IN TIME FOR LUNCH, MOLLY.
I'M... I'M NOT HUNGRY.
I DIDN'T KNOW WHETHER I SHOULD STAY. JUST BEING AROUND HEATHER WAS BEGINNING TO MAKE ME NERVOUS.
WHERE'S MICHAEL?
I SUPPOSE HE'S OUT IN THE WOODS SOMEWHERE.
WHERE ARE YOU GOING, HEATHER?
I'M EATING WITH DADDY.
WHERE WERE YOU ALL MORNING? WERE YOU WITH HEATHER?
I TRIED TO THINK OF AN ANSWER THAT WOULDN'T GET ME INTO TROUBLE.
WE... WE WERE OUT IN THE WOODS.
THERE'S AN OLD HOUSE WAY DOWN THE CREEK-- JUST RUINS, REALLY-- AND A POND.
HEATHER LOVES GOING THERE, BUT I THINK IT'S KIND OF DANGEROUS.
I DIDN'T KNOW THERE WERE ANY OLD HOUSES NEARBY.

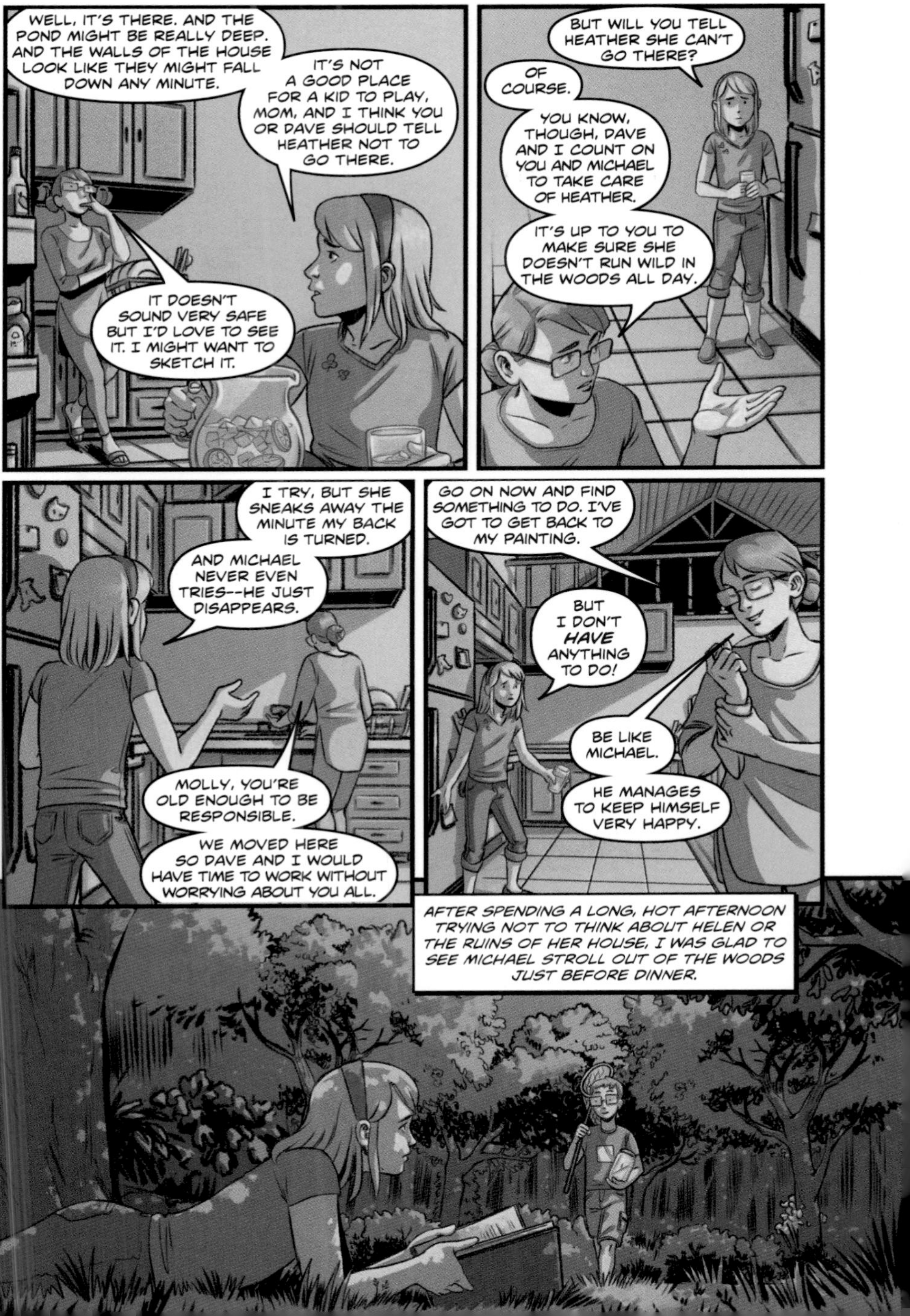
WELL, IT'S THERE. AND THE POND MIGHT BE REALLY DEEP. AND THE WALLS OF THE HOUSE LOOK LIKE THEY MIGHT FALL DOWN ANY MINUTE.
IT'S NOT A GOOD PLACE FOR A KID TO PLAY, MOM, AND I THINK YOU OR DAVE SHOULD TELL HEATHER NOT TO GO THERE.
IT DOESN'T SOUND VERY SAFE BUT I'D LOVE TO SEE IT. I MIGHT WANT TO SKETCH IT.
BUT WILL YOU TELL HEATHER SHE CAN'T GO THERE?
OF COURSE.
YOU KNOW, THOUGH, DAVE AND I COUNT ON YOU AND MICHAEL TO TAKE CARE OF HEATHER.
IT'S UP TO YOU TO MAKE SURE SHE DOESN'T RUN WILD IN THE WOODS ALL DAY.
I TRY, BUT SHE SNEAKS AWAY THE MINUTE MY BACK IS TURNED.
AND MICHAEL NEVER EVEN TRIES--HE JUST DISAPPEARS.
MOLLY, YOU'RE OLD ENOUGH TO BE RESPONSIBLE.
WE MOVED HERE SO DAVE AND I WOULD HAVE TIME TO WORK WITHOUT WORRYING ABOUT YOU ALL.
GO ON NOW AND FIND SOMETHING TO DO. I'VE GOT TO GET BACK TO MY PAINTING.
BUT I DON'T ***HAVE*** ANYTHING TO DO!
BE LIKE MICHAEL.
HE MANAGES TO KEEP HIMSELF VERY HAPPY.
AFTER SPENDING A LONG, HOT AFTERNOON TRYING NOT TO THINK ABOUT HELEN OR THE RUINS OF HER HOUSE, I WAS GLAD TO SEE MICHAEL STROLL OUT OF THE WOODS JUST BEFORE DINNER.

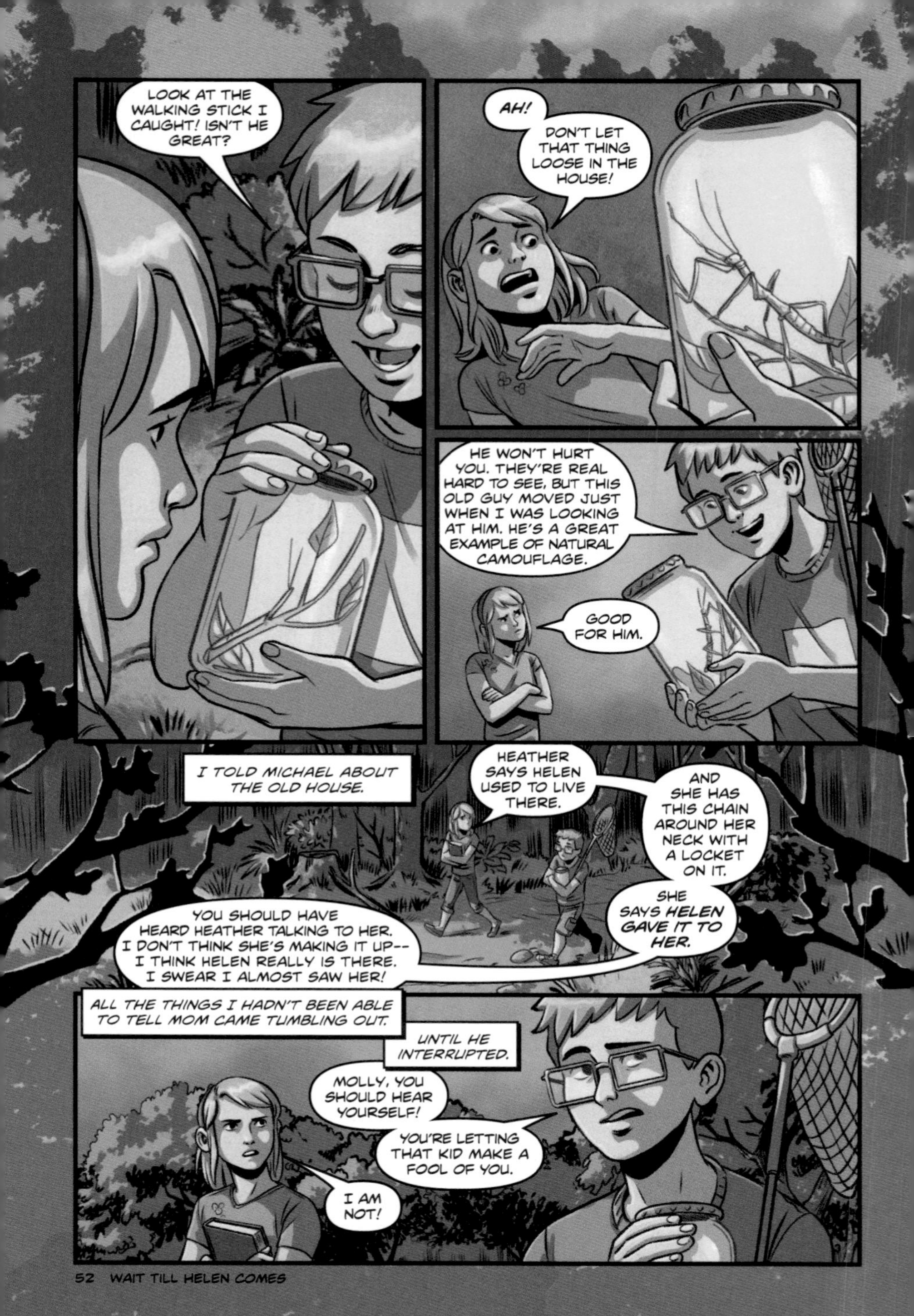
LOOK AT THE WALKING STICK I CAUGHT! ISN'T HE GREAT?
AH!
DON'T LET THAT THING LOOSE IN THE HOUSE!
HE WON'T HURT YOU. THEY'RE REAL HARD TO SEE, BUT THIS OLD GUY MOVED JUST WHEN I WAS LOOKING AT HIM. HE'S A GREAT EXAMPLE OF NATURAL CAMOUFLAGE.
GOOD FOR HIM.
I TOLD MICHAEL ABOUT THE OLD HOUSE.
HEATHER SAYS HELEN USED TO LIVE THERE.
AND SHE HAS THIS CHAIN AROUND HER NECK WITH A LOCKET ON IT.
SHE SAYS HELEN GAVE IT TO HER.
YOU SHOULD HAVE HEARD HEATHER TALKING TO HER. I DON'T THINK SHE'S MAKING IT UP-- I THINK HELEN REALLY IS THERE. I SWEAR I ALMOST SAW HER!
ALL THE THINGS I HADN'T BEEN ABLE TO TELL MOM CAME TUMBLING OUT.
UNTIL HE INTERRUPTED.
MOLLY, YOU SHOULD HEAR YOURSELF!
YOU'RE LETTING THAT KID MAKE A FOOL OF YOU.
I AM NOT!

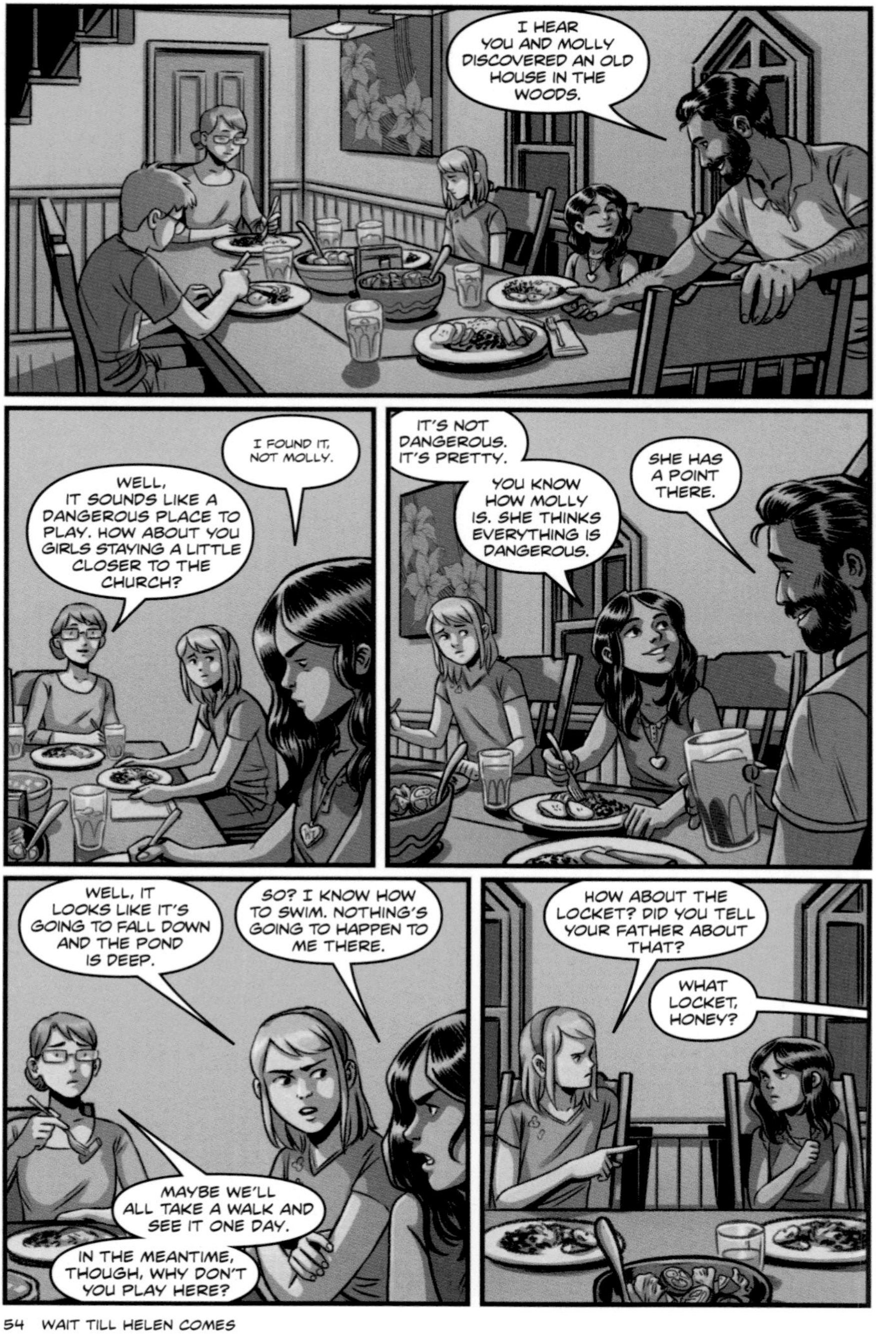

I HEAR YOU AND MOLLY DISCOVERED AN OLD HOUSE IN THE WOODS.
I FOUND IT, NOT MOLLY.
WELL, IT SOUNDS LIKE A DANGEROUS PLACE TO PLAY. HOW ABOUT YOU GIRLS STAYING A LITTLE CLOSER TO THE CHURCH?
IT'S NOT DANGEROUS. IT'S PRETTY.
YOU KNOW HOW MOLLY IS. SHE THINKS EVERYTHING IS DANGEROUS.
SHE HAS A POINT THERE.
WELL, IT LOOKS LIKE IT'S GOING TO FALL DOWN AND THE POND IS DEEP.
SO? I KNOW HOW TO SWIM. NOTHING'S GOING TO HAPPEN TO ME THERE.
MAYBE WE'LL ALL TAKE A WALK AND SEE IT ONE DAY.
IN THE MEANTIME, THOUGH, WHY DON'T YOU PLAY HERE?
HOW ABOUT THE LOCKET? DID YOU TELL YOUR FATHER ABOUT THAT?
WHAT LOCKET, HONEY?

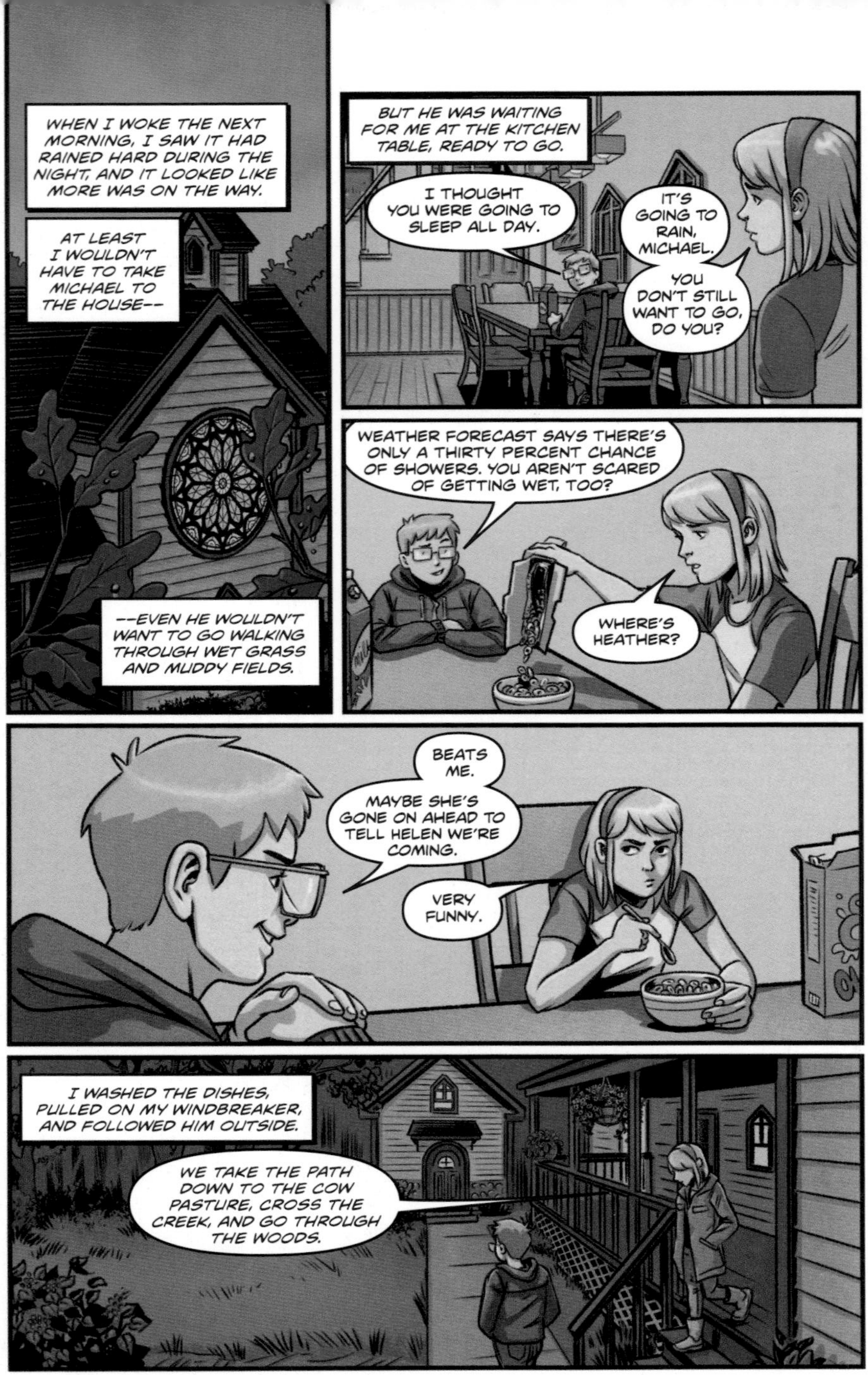
WHEN I WOKE THE NEXT MORNING, I SAW IT HAD RAINED HARD DURING THE NIGHT, AND IT LOOKED LIKE MORE WAS ON THE WAY.
AT LEAST I WOULDN'T HAVE TO TAKE MICHAEL TO THE HOUSE--
--EVEN HE WOULDN'T WANT TO GO WALKING THROUGH WET GRASS AND MUDDY FIELDS.
BUT HE WAS WAITING FOR ME AT THE KITCHEN TABLE, READY TO GO.
I THOUGHT YOU WERE GOING TO SLEEP ALL DAY.
IT'S GOING TO RAIN, MICHAEL.
YOU DON'T STILL WANT TO GO, DO YOU?
WEATHER FORECAST SAYS THERE'S ONLY A THIRTY PERCENT CHANCE OF SHOWERS. YOU AREN'T SCARED OF GETTING WET, TOO?
WHERE'S HEATHER?
BEATS ME.
MAYBE SHE'S GONE ON AHEAD TO TELL HELEN WE'RE COMING.
VERY FUNNY.
I WASHED THE DISHES, PULLED ON MY WINDBREAKER, AND FOLLOWED HIM OUTSIDE.
WE TAKE THE PATH DOWN TO THE COW PASTURE, CROSS THE CREEK, AND GO THROUGH THE WOODS.

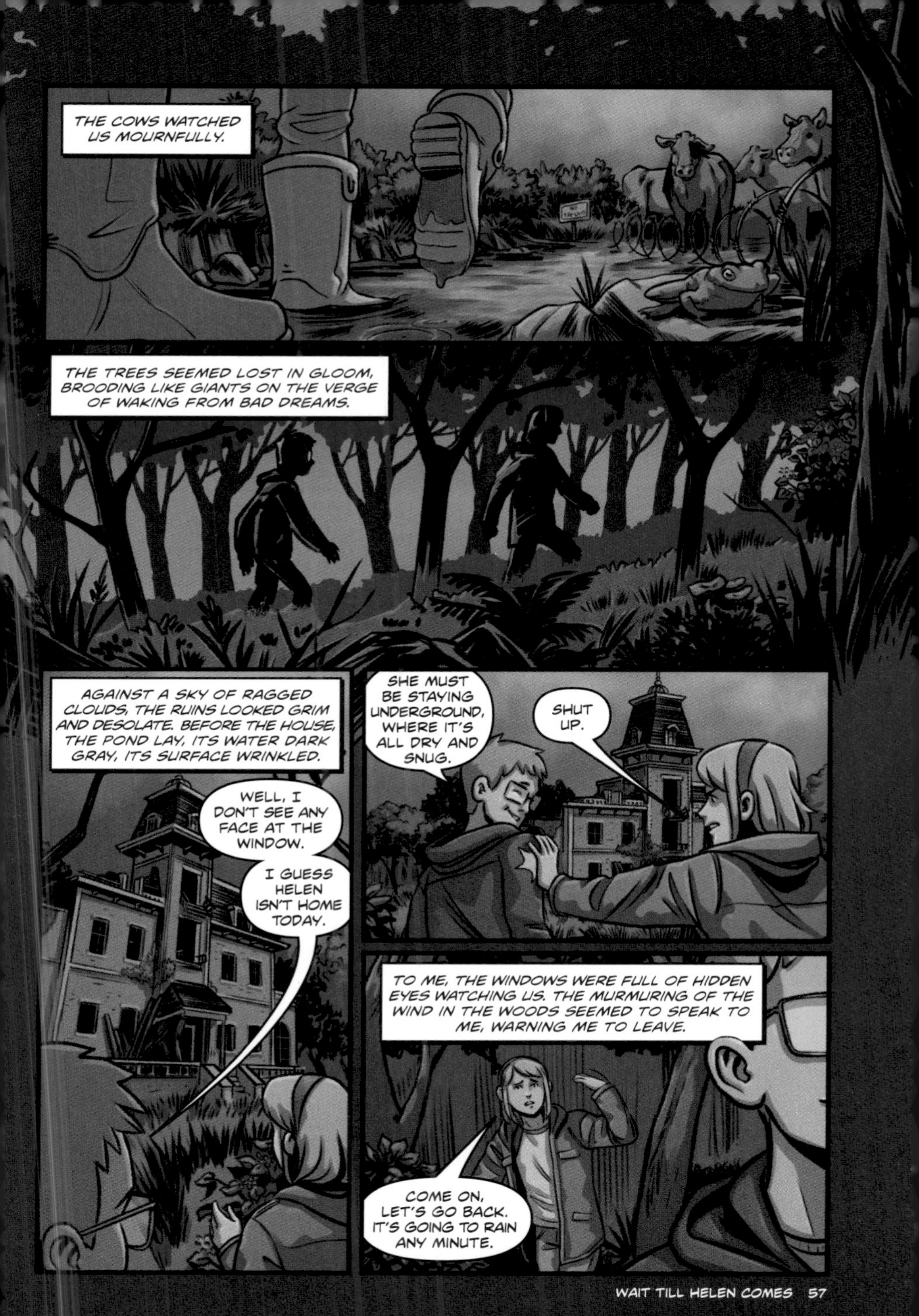
THE COWS WATCHED US MOURNFULLY.
THE TREES SEEMED LOST IN GLOOM, BROODING LIKE GIANTS ON THE VERGE OF WAKING FROM BAD DREAMS.
AGAINST A SKY OF RAGGED CLOUDS, THE RUINS LOOKED GRIM AND DESOLATE. BEFORE THE HOUSE, THE POND LAY, ITS WATER DARK GRAY, ITS SURFACE WRINKLED.
WELL, I DON'T SEE ANY FACE AT THE WINDOW.
I GUESS HELEN ISN'T HOME TODAY.
SHE MUST BE STAYING UNDERGROUND, WHERE IT'S ALL DRY AND SNUG.
SHUT UP.
TO ME, THE WINDOWS WERE FULL OF HIDDEN EYES WATCHING US. THE MURMURING OF THE WIND IN THE WOODS SEEMED TO SPEAK TO ME, WARNING ME TO LEAVE.
COME ON, LET'S GO BACK. IT'S GOING TO RAIN ANY MINUTE.

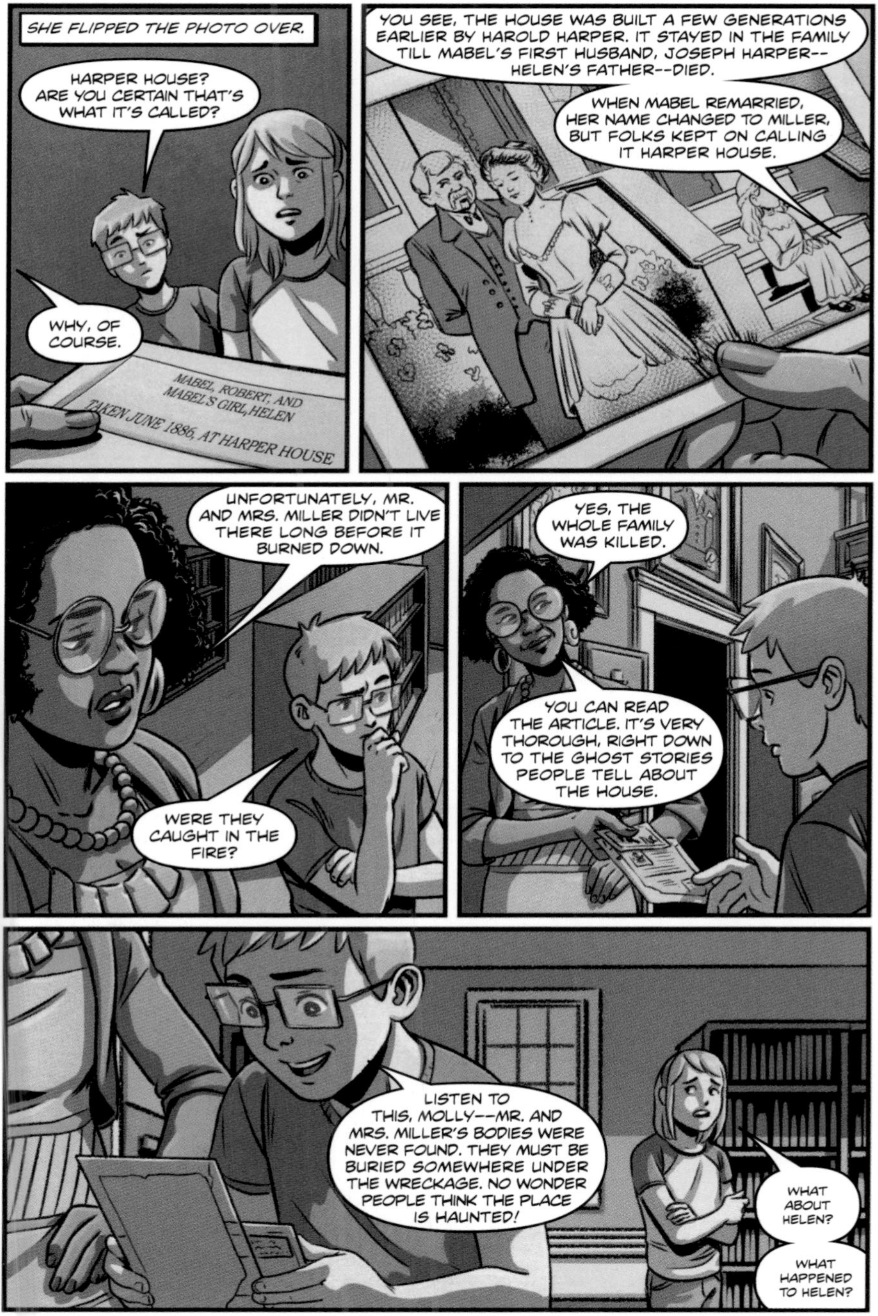
SHE FLIPPED THE PHOTO OVER.
HARPER HOUSE? ARE YOU CERTAIN THAT'S WHAT IT'S CALLED?
WHY, OF COURSE.
MABEL, ROBERT, AND MABEL'S GIRL, HELEN
TAKEN JUNE 1886, AT HARPER HOUSE
YOU SEE, THE HOUSE WAS BUILT A FEW GENERATIONS EARLIER BY HAROLD HARPER. IT STAYED IN THE FAMILY TILL MABEL'S FIRST HUSBAND, JOSEPH HARPER--HELEN'S FATHER--DIED.
WHEN MABEL REMARRIED, HER NAME CHANGED TO MILLER, BUT FOLKS KEPT ON CALLING IT HARPER HOUSE.
UNFORTUNATELY, MR. AND MRS. MILLER DIDN'T LIVE THERE LONG BEFORE IT BURNED DOWN.
WERE THEY CAUGHT IN THE FIRE?
YES, THE WHOLE FAMILY WAS KILLED.
YOU CAN READ THE ARTICLE. IT'S VERY THOROUGH, RIGHT DOWN TO THE GHOST STORIES PEOPLE TELL ABOUT THE HOUSE.
LISTEN TO THIS, MOLLY--MR. AND MRS. MILLER'S BODIES WERE NEVER FOUND. THEY MUST BE BURIED SOMEWHERE UNDER THE WRECKAGE. NO WONDER PEOPLE THINK THE PLACE IS HAUNTED!
WHAT ABOUT HELEN?
WHAT HAPPENED TO HELEN?

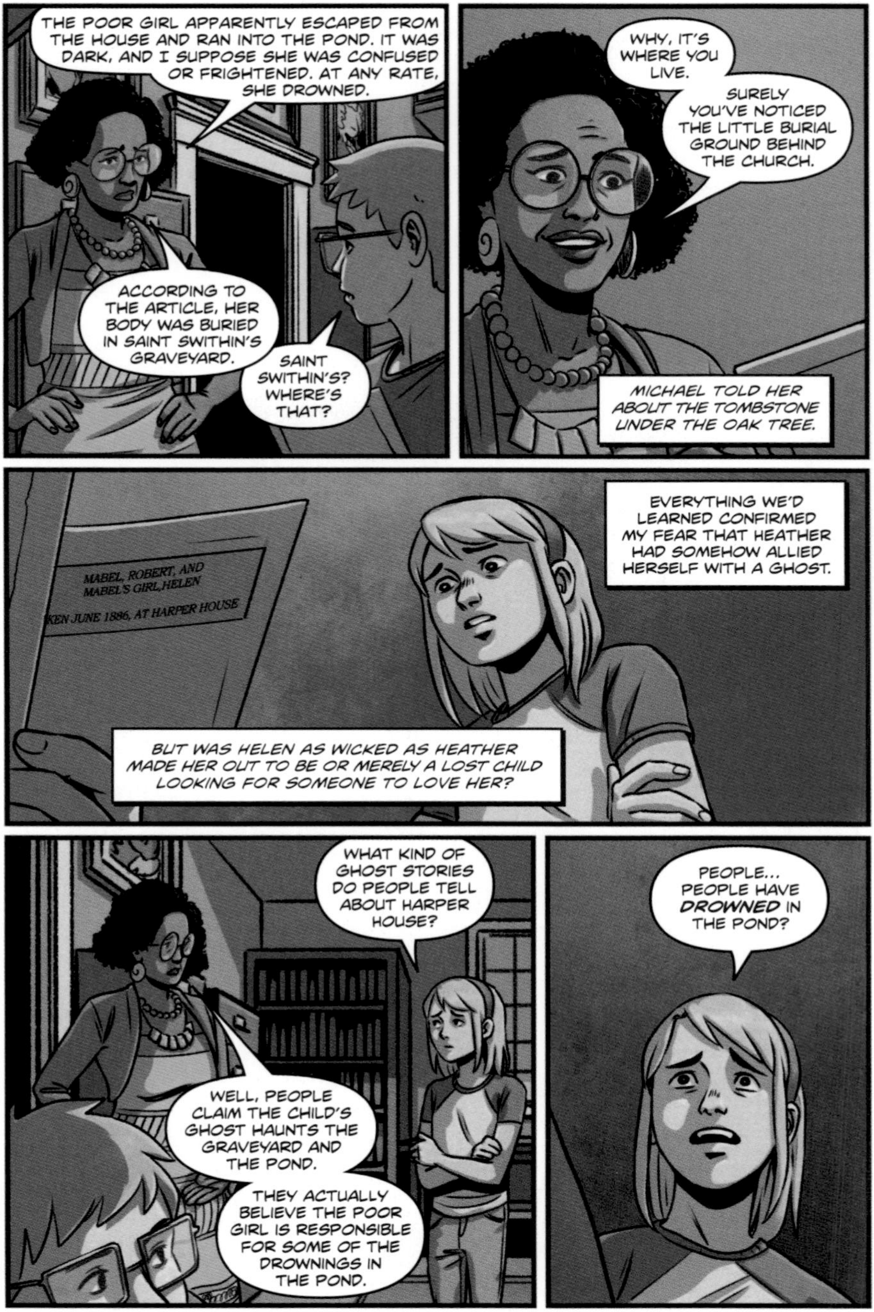
THE POOR GIRL APPARENTLY ESCAPED FROM THE HOUSE AND RAN INTO THE POND. IT WAS DARK, AND I SUPPOSE SHE WAS CONFUSED OR FRIGHTENED. AT ANY RATE, SHE DROWNED.
ACCORDING TO THE ARTICLE, HER BODY WAS BURIED IN SAINT SWITHIN'S GRAVEYARD.
SAINT SWITHIN'S? WHERE'S THAT?
WHY, IT'S WHERE YOU LIVE.
SURELY YOU'VE NOTICED THE LITTLE BURIAL GROUND BEHIND THE CHURCH.
MICHAEL TOLD HER ABOUT THE TOMBSTONE UNDER THE OAK TREE.
EVERYTHING WE'D LEARNED CONFIRMED MY FEAR THAT HEATHER HAD SOMEHOW ALLIED HERSELF WITH A GHOST.
MABEL, ROBERT, AND MABEL'S GIRL, HELEN
KEN JUNE 1886, AT HARPER HOUSE
BUT WAS HELEN AS WICKED AS HEATHER MADE HER OUT TO BE OR MERELY A LOST CHILD LOOKING FOR SOMEONE TO LOVE HER?
WHAT KIND OF GHOST STORIES DO PEOPLE TELL ABOUT HARPER HOUSE?
WELL, PEOPLE CLAIM THE CHILD'S GHOST HAUNTS THE GRAVEYARD AND THE POND.
THEY ACTUALLY BELIEVE THE POOR GIRL IS RESPONSIBLE FOR SOME OF THE DROWNINGS IN THE POND.
PEOPLE... PEOPLE HAVE ***DROWNED*** IN THE POND?

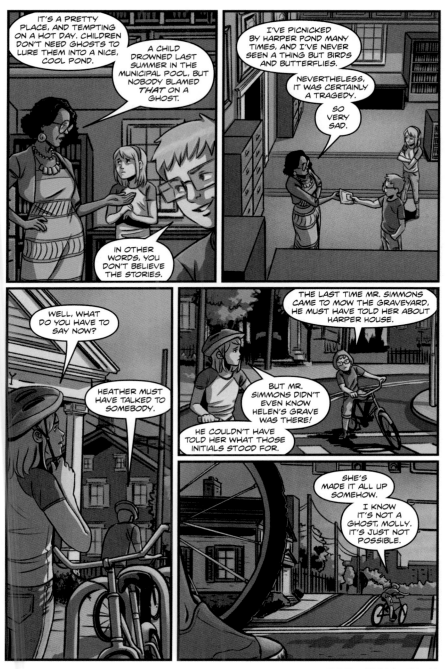

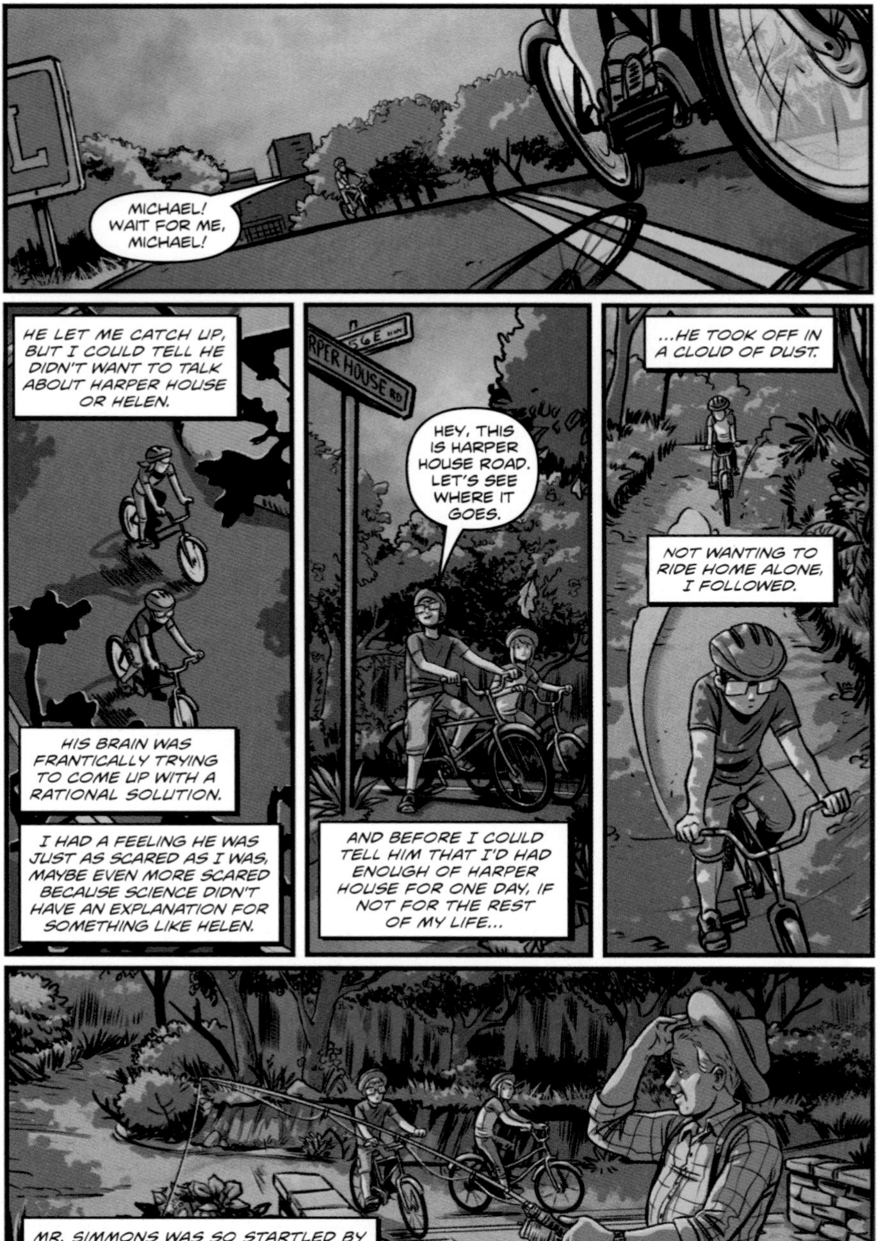
MICHAEL! WAIT FOR ME, MICHAEL!
HE LET ME CATCH UP, BUT I COULD TELL HE DIDN'T WANT TO TALK ABOUT HARPER HOUSE OR HELEN.
HIS BRAIN WAS FRANTICALLY TRYING TO COME UP WITH A RATIONAL SOLUTION.
I HAD A FEELING HE WAS JUST AS SCARED AS I WAS, MAYBE EVEN MORE SCARED BECAUSE SCIENCE DIDN'T HAVE AN EXPLANATION FOR SOMETHING LIKE HELEN.
HEY, THIS IS HARPER HOUSE ROAD. LET'S SEE WHERE IT GOES.
AND BEFORE I COULD TELL HIM THAT I'D HAD ENOUGH OF HARPER HOUSE FOR ONE DAY, IF NOT FOR THE REST OF MY LIFE...
...HE TOOK OFF IN A CLOUD OF DUST.
NOT WANTING TO RIDE HOME ALONE, I FOLLOWED.
MR. SIMMONS WAS SO STARTLED BY OUR SUDDEN APPEARANCE THAT HE ALMOST DROPPED HIS FISHING POLE.

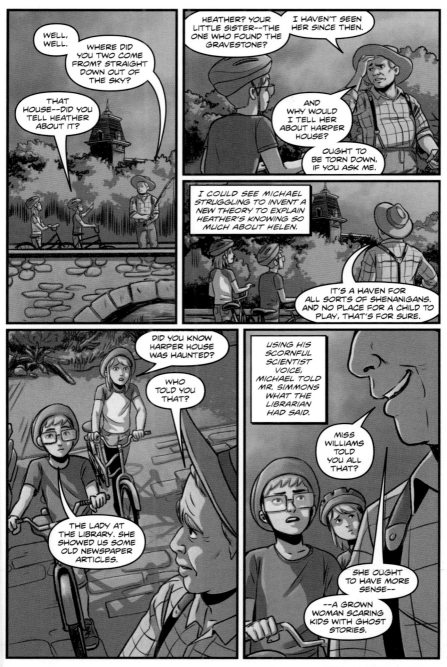

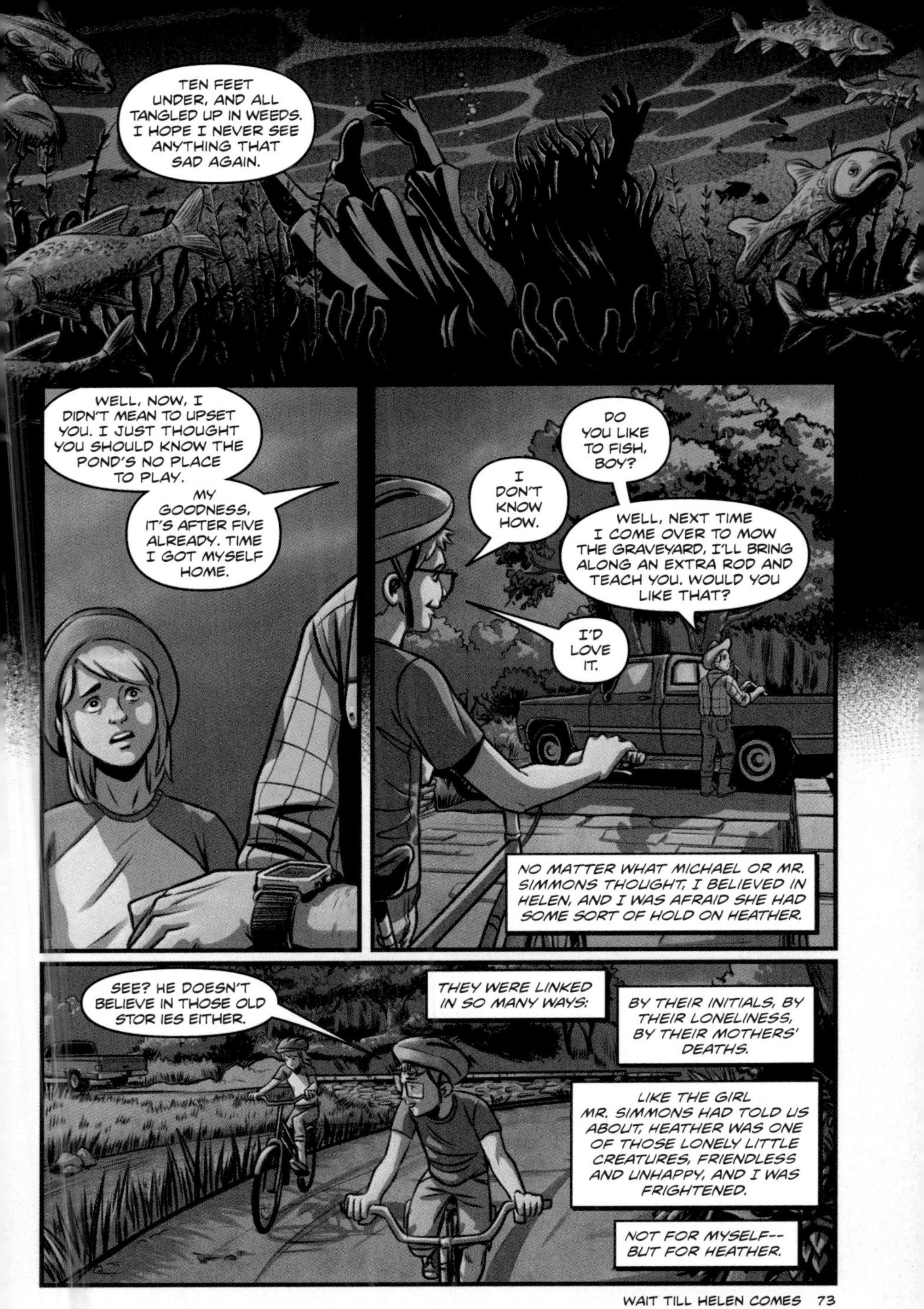
TEN FEET UNDER, AND ALL TANGLED UP IN WEEDS. I HOPE I NEVER SEE ANYTHING THAT SAD AGAIN.
WELL, NOW, I DIDN'T MEAN TO UPSET YOU. I JUST THOUGHT YOU SHOULD KNOW THE POND'S NO PLACE TO PLAY.
MY GOODNESS, IT'S AFTER FIVE ALREADY. TIME I GOT MYSELF HOME.
DO YOU LIKE TO FISH, BOY?
I DON'T KNOW HOW.
WELL, NEXT TIME I COME OVER TO MOW THE GRAVEYARD, I'LL BRING ALONG AN EXTRA ROD AND TEACH YOU. WOULD YOU LIKE THAT?
I'D LOVE IT.
NO MATTER WHAT MICHAEL OR MR. SIMMONS THOUGHT, I BELIEVED IN HELEN, AND I WAS AFRAID SHE HAD SOME SORT OF HOLD ON HEATHER.
SEE? HE DOESN'T BELIEVE IN THOSE OLD STOR IES EITHER.
THEY WERE LINKED IN SO MANY WAYS:
BY THEIR INITIALS, BY THEIR LONELINESS, BY THEIR MOTHERS' DEATHS.
LIKE THE GIRL MR. SIMMONS HAD TOLD US ABOUT, HEATHER WAS ONE OF THOSE LONELY LITTLE CREATURES, FRIENDLESS AND UNHAPPY, AND I WAS FRIGHTENED.
NOT FOR MYSELF-- BUT FOR HEATHER.

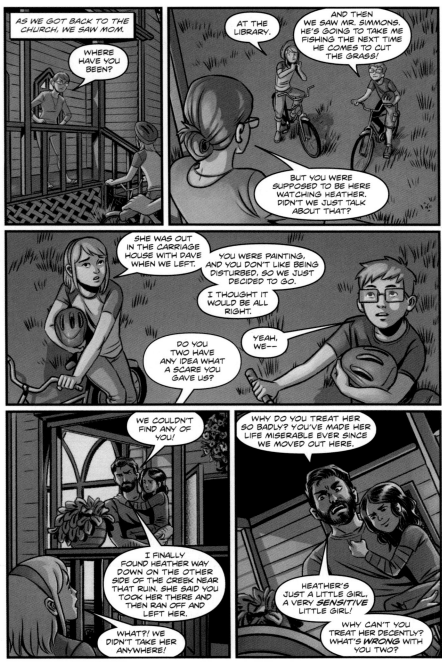

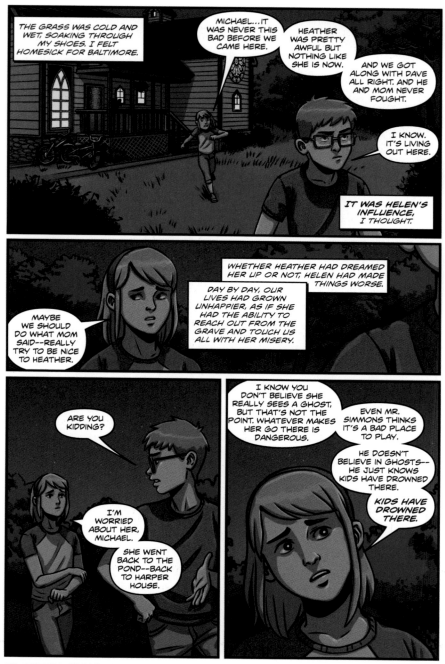

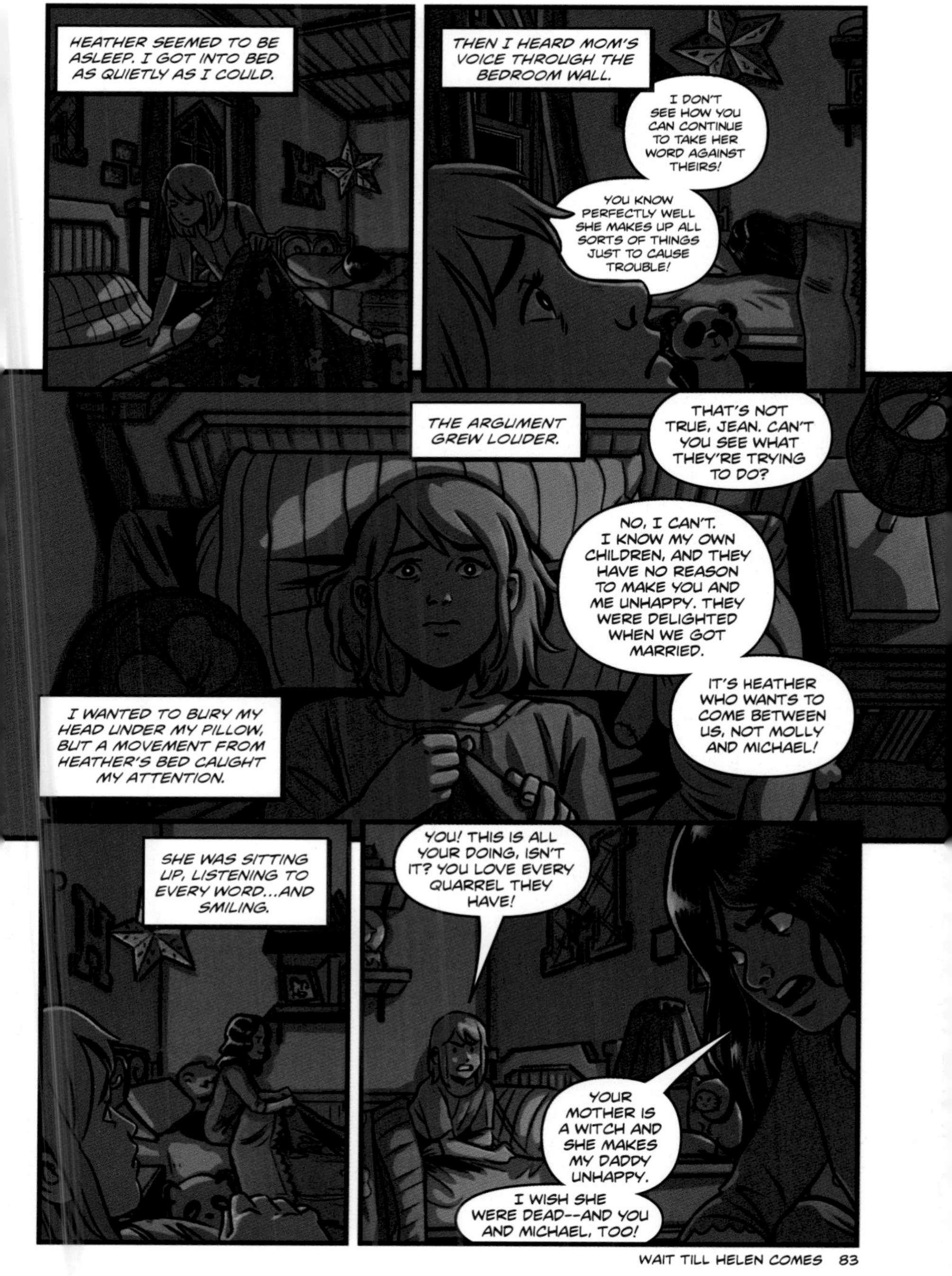
HEATHER SEEMED TO BE ASLEEP. I GOT INTO BED AS QUIETLY AS I COULD.
THEN I HEARD MOM'S VOICE THROUGH THE BEDROOM WALL.
I DON'T SEE HOW YOU CAN CONTINUE TO TAKE HER WORD AGAINST THEIRS!
YOU KNOW PERFECTLY WELL SHE MAKES UP ALL SORTS OF THINGS JUST TO CAUSE TROUBLE!
THE ARGUMENT GREW LOUDER.
THAT'S NOT TRUE, JEAN. CAN'T YOU SEE WHAT THEY'RE TRYING TO DO?
NO, I CAN'T. I KNOW MY OWN CHILDREN, AND THEY HAVE NO REASON TO MAKE YOU AND ME UNHAPPY. THEY WERE DELIGHTED WHEN WE GOT MARRIED.
IT'S HEATHER WHO WANTS TO COME BETWEEN US, NOT MOLLY AND MICHAEL!
I WANTED TO BURY MY HEAD UNDER MY PILLOW, BUT A MOVEMENT FROM HEATHER'S BED CAUGHT MY ATTENTION.
SHE WAS SITTING UP, LISTENING TO EVERY WORD...AND SMILING.
YOU! THIS IS ALL YOUR DOING, ISN'T IT? YOU LOVE EVERY QUARREL THEY HAVE!
YOUR MOTHER IS A WITCH AND SHE MAKES MY DADDY UNHAPPY.
I WISH SHE WERE DEAD--AND YOU AND MICHAEL, TOO!

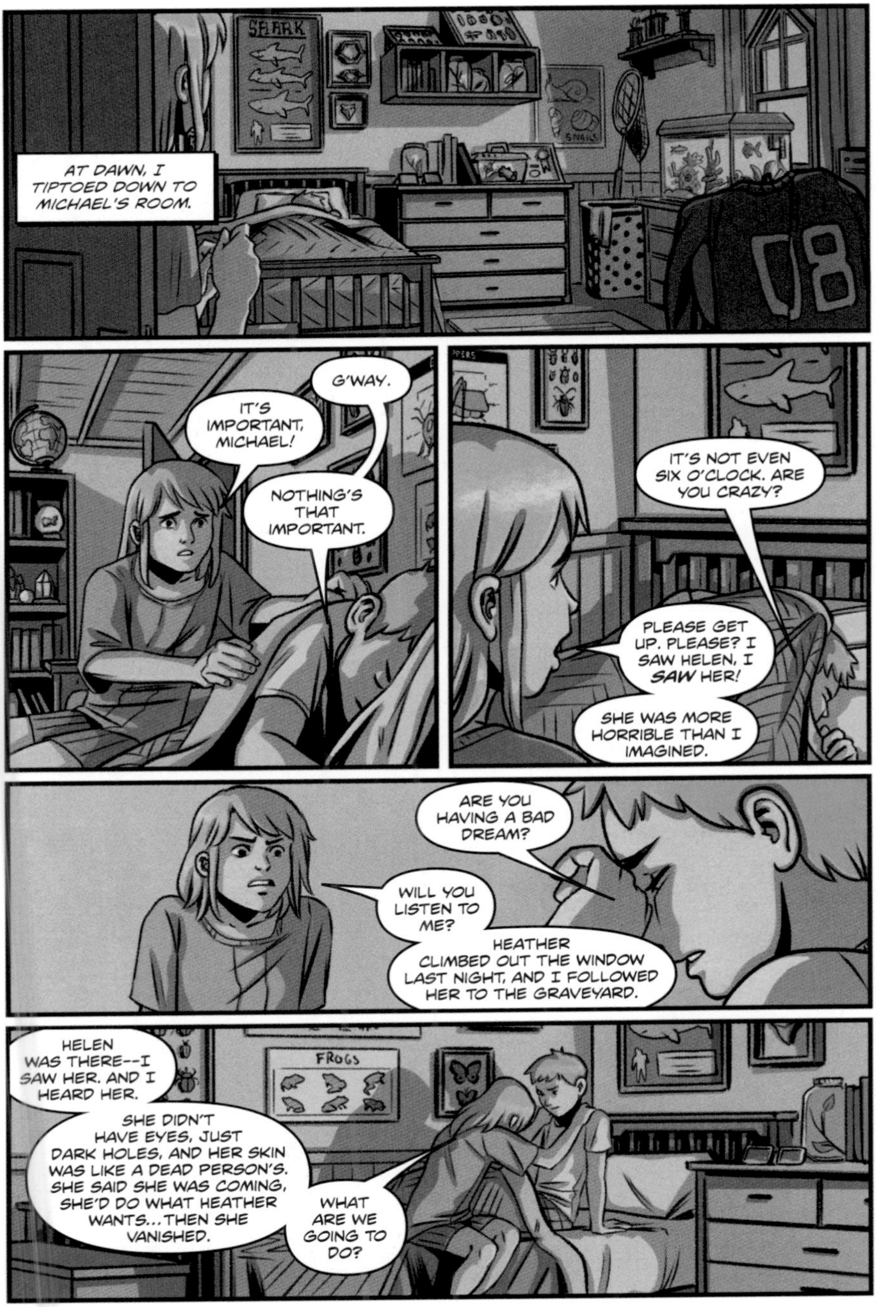
AT DAWN, I TIPTOED DOWN TO MICHAEL'S ROOM.
IT'S IMPORTANT, MICHAEL!
G'WAY.
NOTHING'S THAT IMPORTANT.
IT'S NOT EVEN SIX O'CLOCK. ARE YOU CRAZY?
PLEASE GET UP. PLEASE? I SAW HELEN, I *SAW* HER!
SHE WAS MORE HORRIBLE THAN I IMAGINED.
ARE YOU HAVING A BAD DREAM?
WILL YOU LISTEN TO ME?
HEATHER CLIMBED OUT THE WINDOW LAST NIGHT, AND I FOLLOWED HER TO THE GRAVEYARD.
HELEN WAS THERE--I SAW HER. AND I HEARD HER.
SHE DIDN'T HAVE EYES, JUST DARK HOLES, AND HER SKIN WAS LIKE A DEAD PERSON'S. SHE SAID SHE WAS COMING, SHE'D DO WHAT HEATHER WANTS... THEN SHE VANISHED.
WHAT ARE WE GOING TO DO?

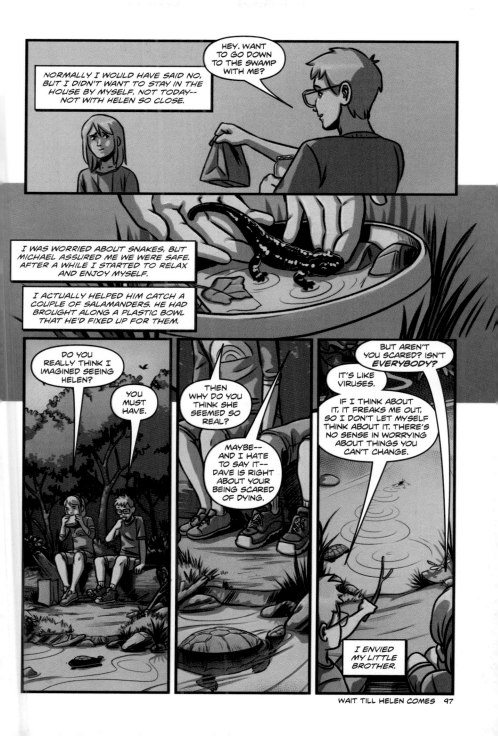

NORMALLY I WOULD HAVE SAID NO, BUT I DIDN'T WANT TO STAY IN THE HOUSE BY MYSELF. NOT TODAY-- NOT WITH HELEN SO CLOSE.

HEY. WANT TO GO DOWN TO THE SWAMP WITH ME?

I WAS WORRIED ABOUT SNAKES, BUT MICHAEL ASSURED ME WE WERE SAFE. AFTER A WHILE I STARTED TO RELAX AND ENJOY MYSELF.

I ACTUALLY HELPED HIM CATCH A COUPLE OF SALAMANDERS. HE HAD BROUGHT ALONG A PLASTIC BOWL THAT HE'D FIXED UP FOR THEM.

DO YOU REALLY THINK I IMAGINED SEEING HELEN?

YOU MUST HAVE.

THEN WHY DO YOU THINK SHE SEEMED SO REAL?

MAYBE-- AND I HATE TO SAY IT-- DAVE IS RIGHT ABOUT YOUR BEING SCARED OF DYING.

BUT AREN'T YOU SCARED? ISN'T EVERYBODY?

IT'S LIKE VIRUSES.

IF I THINK ABOUT IT, IT FREAKS ME OUT, SO I DON'T LET MYSELF THINK ABOUT IT. THERE'S NO SENSE IN WORRYING ABOUT THINGS YOU CAN'T CHANGE.

I ENVIED MY LITTLE BROTHER.

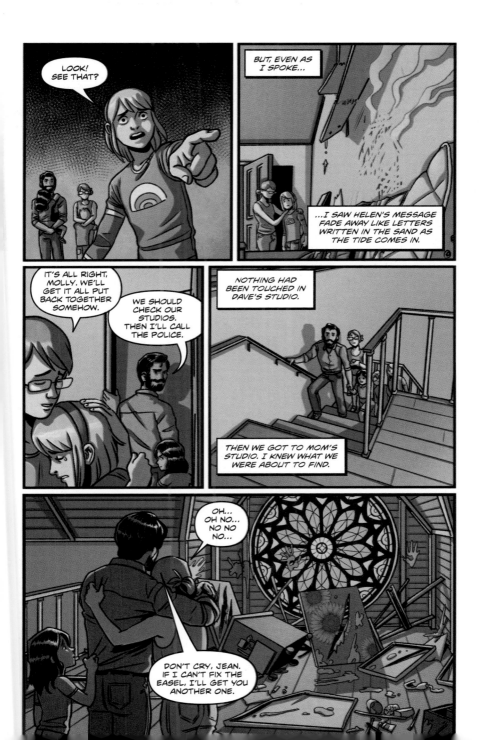

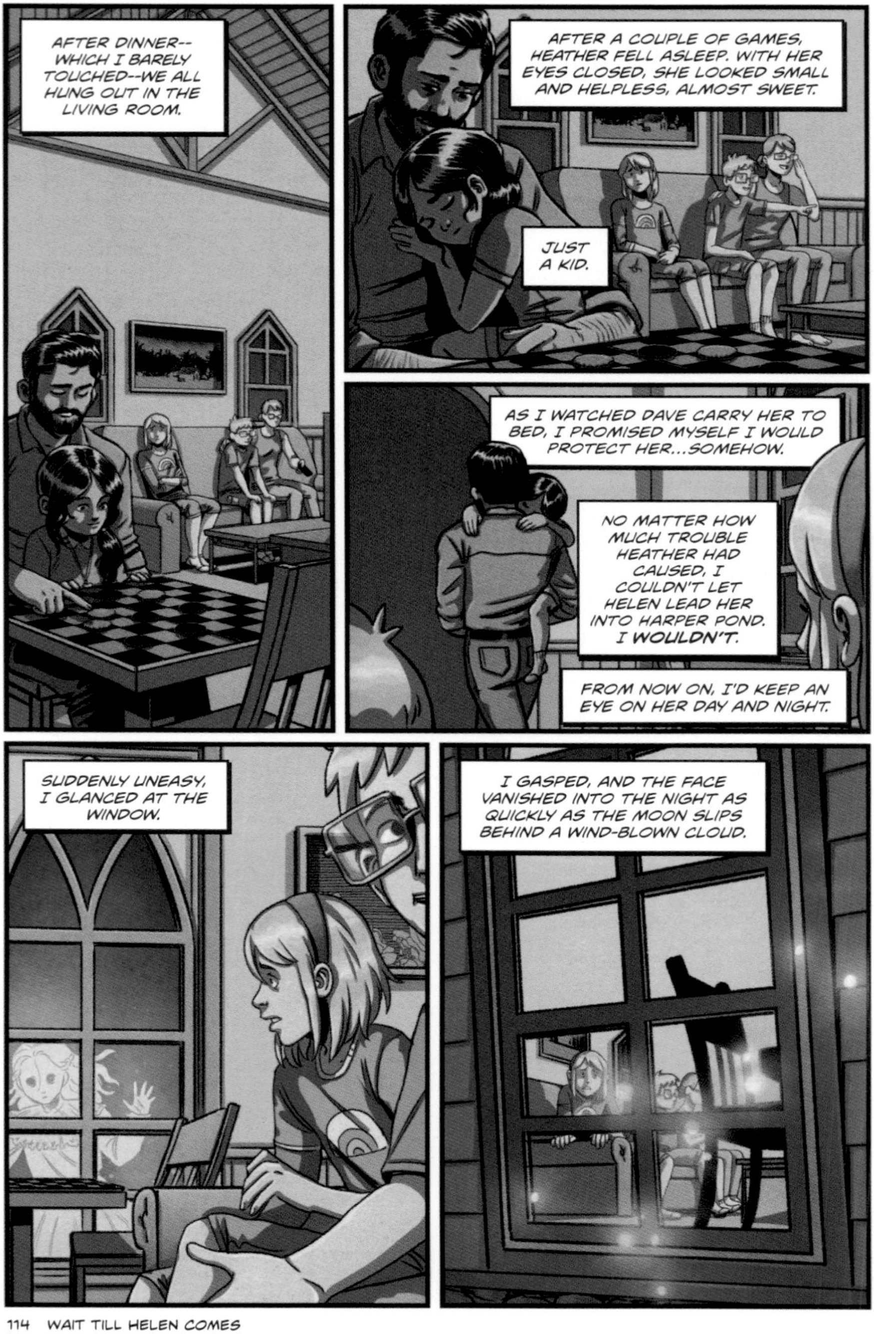
AFTER DINNER--WHICH I BARELY TOUCHED--WE ALL HUNG OUT IN THE LIVING ROOM.
AFTER A COUPLE OF GAMES, HEATHER FELL ASLEEP. WITH HER EYES CLOSED, SHE LOOKED SMALL AND HELPLESS, ALMOST SWEET.
JUST A KID.
AS I WATCHED DAVE CARRY HER TO BED, I PROMISED MYSELF I WOULD PROTECT HER...SOMEHOW.
NO MATTER HOW MUCH TROUBLE HEATHER HAD CAUSED, I COULDN'T LET HELEN LEAD HER INTO HARPER POND. I **WOULDN'T**.
FROM NOW ON, I'D KEEP AN EYE ON HER DAY AND NIGHT.
SUDDENLY UNEASY, I GLANCED AT THE WINDOW.
I GASPED, AND THE FACE VANISHED INTO THE NIGHT AS QUICKLY AS THE MOON SLIPS BEHIND A WIND-BLOWN CLOUD.

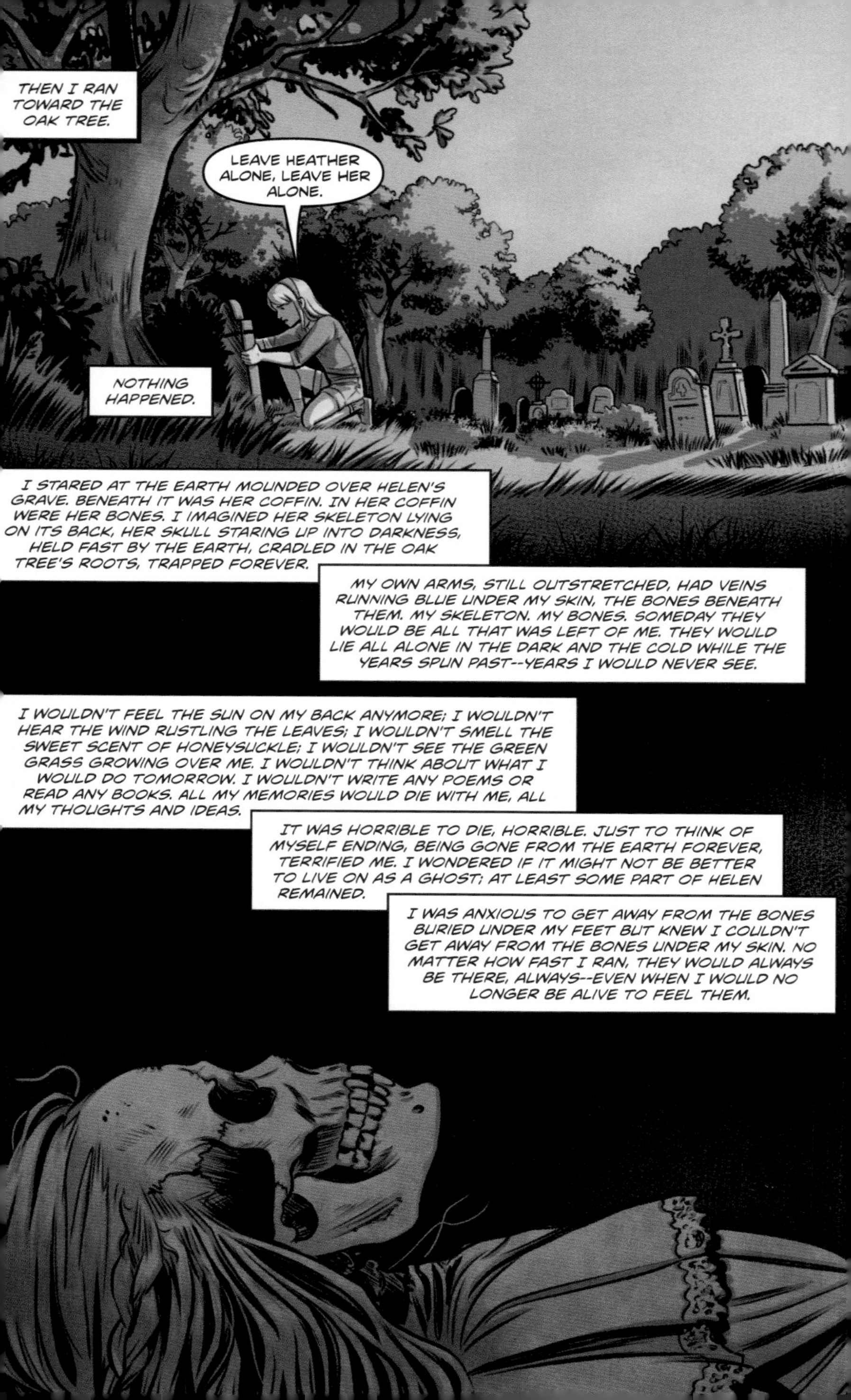
THEN I RAN TOWARD THE OAK TREE.
LEAVE HEATHER ALONE, LEAVE HER ALONE.
NOTHING HAPPENED.
I STARED AT THE EARTH MOUNDED OVER HELEN'S GRAVE. BENEATH IT WAS HER COFFIN. IN HER COFFIN WERE HER BONES. I IMAGINED HER SKELETON LYING ON ITS BACK, HER SKULL STARING UP INTO DARKNESS, HELD FAST BY THE EARTH, CRADLED IN THE OAK TREE'S ROOTS, TRAPPED FOREVER.
MY OWN ARMS, STILL OUTSTRETCHED, HAD VEINS RUNNING BLUE UNDER MY SKIN, THE BONES BENEATH THEM. MY SKELETON. MY BONES. SOMEDAY THEY WOULD BE ALL THAT WAS LEFT OF ME. THEY WOULD LIE ALL ALONE IN THE DARK AND THE COLD WHILE THE YEARS SPUN PAST--YEARS I WOULD NEVER SEE.
I WOULDN'T FEEL THE SUN ON MY BACK ANYMORE; I WOULDN'T HEAR THE WIND RUSTLING THE LEAVES; I WOULDN'T SMELL THE SWEET SCENT OF HONEYSUCKLE; I WOULDN'T SEE THE GREEN GRASS GROWING OVER ME. I WOULDN'T THINK ABOUT WHAT I WOULD DO TOMORROW. I WOULDN'T WRITE ANY POEMS OR READ ANY BOOKS. ALL MY MEMORIES WOULD DIE WITH ME, ALL MY THOUGHTS AND IDEAS.
IT WAS HORRIBLE TO DIE, HORRIBLE. JUST TO THINK OF MYSELF ENDING, BEING GONE FROM THE EARTH FOREVER, TERRIFIED ME. I WONDERED IF IT MIGHT NOT BE BETTER TO LIVE ON AS A GHOST; AT LEAST SOME PART OF HELEN REMAINED.
I WAS ANXIOUS TO GET AWAY FROM THE BONES BURIED UNDER MY FEET BUT KNEW I COULDN'T GET AWAY FROM THE BONES UNDER MY SKIN. NO MATTER HOW FAST I RAN, THEY WOULD ALWAYS BE THERE, ALWAYS--EVEN WHEN I WOULD NO LONGER BE ALIVE TO FEEL THEM.

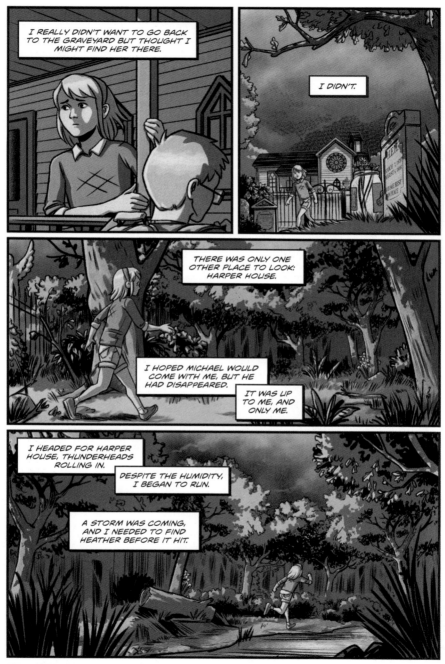

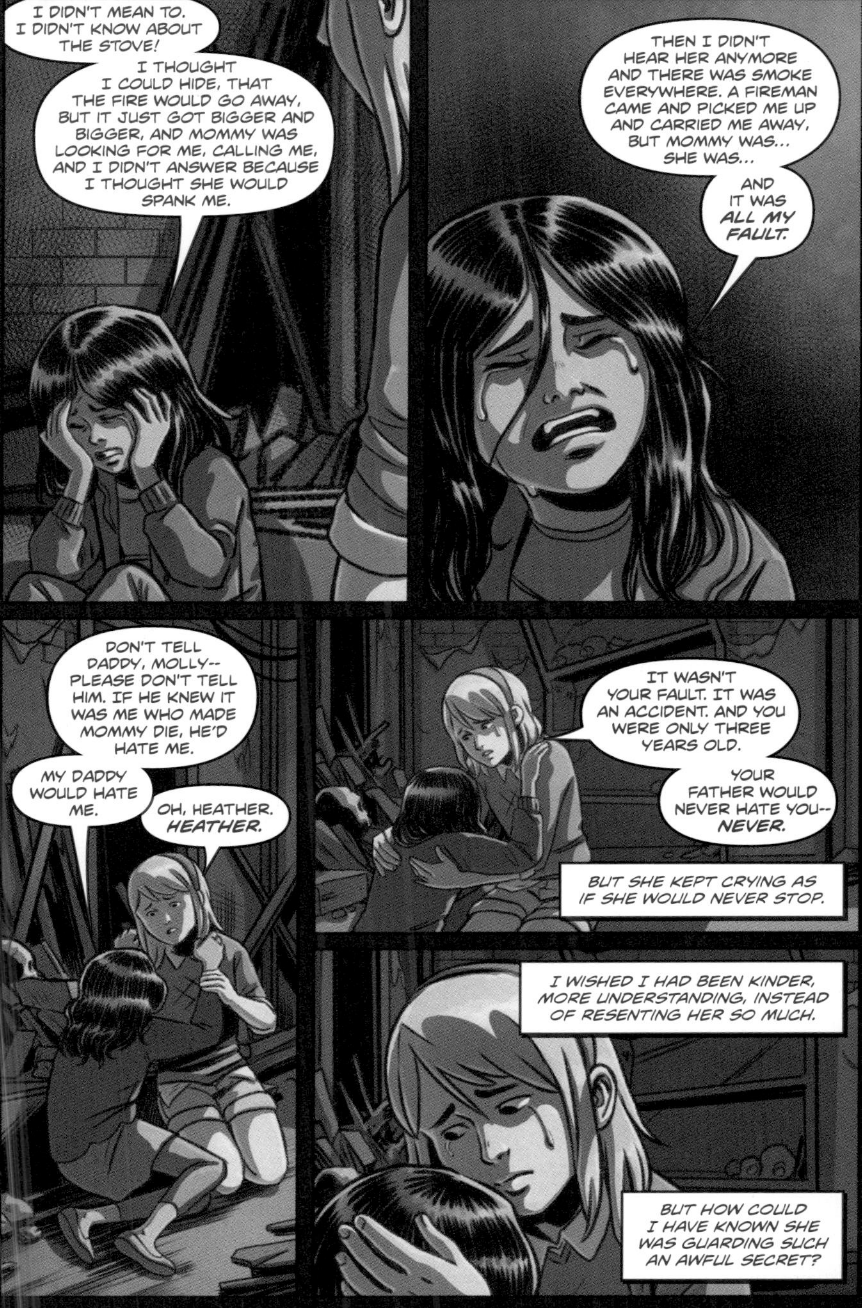
I DIDN'T MEAN TO. I DIDN'T KNOW ABOUT THE STOVE!
I THOUGHT I COULD HIDE, THAT THE FIRE WOULD GO AWAY, BUT IT JUST GOT BIGGER AND BIGGER, AND MOMMY WAS LOOKING FOR ME, CALLING ME, AND I DIDN'T ANSWER BECAUSE I THOUGHT SHE WOULD SPANK ME.
THEN I DIDN'T HEAR HER ANYMORE AND THERE WAS SMOKE EVERYWHERE. A FIREMAN CAME AND PICKED ME UP AND CARRIED ME AWAY, BUT MOMMY WAS... SHE WAS...
AND IT WAS ***ALL MY FAULT.***
DON'T TELL DADDY, MOLLY-- PLEASE DON'T TELL HIM. IF HE KNEW IT WAS ME WHO MADE MOMMY DIE, HE'D HATE ME.
MY DADDY WOULD HATE ME.
OH, HEATHER. ***HEATHER.***
IT WASN'T YOUR FAULT. IT WAS AN ACCIDENT. AND YOU WERE ONLY THREE YEARS OLD.
YOUR FATHER WOULD NEVER HATE YOU-- ***NEVER.***
BUT SHE KEPT CRYING AS IF SHE WOULD NEVER STOP.
I WISHED I HAD BEEN KINDER, MORE UNDERSTANDING, INSTEAD OF RESENTING HER SO MUCH.
BUT HOW COULD I HAVE KNOWN SHE WAS GUARDING SUCH AN AWFUL SECRET?

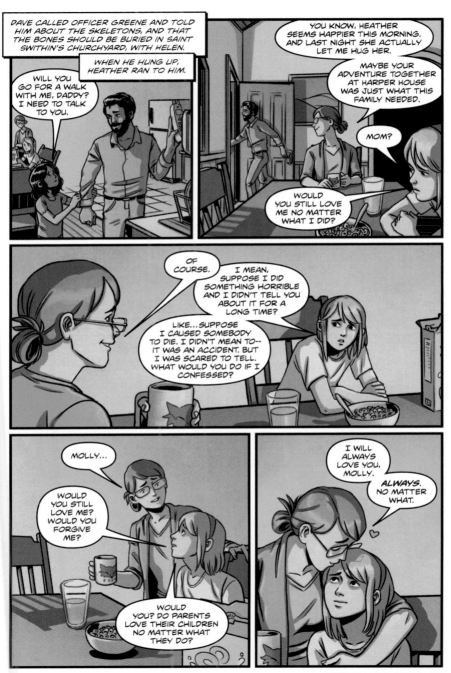

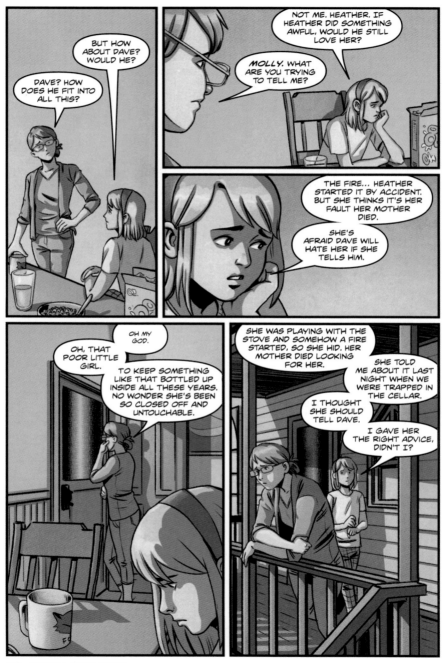

DAVE? HOW DOES HE FIT INTO ALL THIS?

BUT HOW ABOUT DAVE? WOULD HE?

NOT ME. HEATHER. IF HEATHER DID SOMETHING AWFUL, WOULD HE STILL LOVE HER?

MOLLY. WHAT ARE YOU TRYING TO TELL ME?

THE FIRE... HEATHER STARTED IT BY ACCIDENT. BUT SHE THINKS IT'S HER FAULT HER MOTHER DIED.

SHE'S AFRAID DAVE WILL HATE HER IF SHE TELLS HIM.

OH MY GOD.

OH, THAT POOR LITTLE GIRL.

TO KEEP SOMETHING LIKE THAT BOTTLED UP INSIDE ALL THESE YEARS. NO WONDER SHE'S BEEN SO CLOSED OFF AND UNTOUCHABLE.

SHE WAS PLAYING WITH THE STOVE AND SOMEHOW A FIRE STARTED, SO SHE HID. HER MOTHER DIED LOOKING FOR HER.

SHE TOLD ME ABOUT IT LAST NIGHT WHEN WE WERE TRAPPED IN THE CELLAR.

I THOUGHT SHE SHOULD TELL DAVE.

I GAVE HER THE RIGHT ADVICE, DIDN'T I?

A FEW DAYS LATER, THERE WAS A FUNERAL IN SAINT SWITHIN'S GRAVEYARD, THE FIRST ONE IN FORTY YEARS.

MR. SIMMONS HIMSELF HAD SUPERVISED THE DIGGING OF THE GRAVES.

A NUMBER OF PEOPLE FROM HOLWELL, INCLUDING A REPORTER FOR THE TRIBUNE, SHOWED UP.

AT THE END OF THE SERVICE, EVERYONE PICKED UP A HANDFUL OF EARTH AND TOSSED IT INTO THE GRAVES.

A FEW COMMENTED ON HEATHER'S TEARS.

YOU'D THINK SHE KNEW THE POOR SOULS PERSONALLY.

SHE'S TOO YOUNG TO BE EXPOSED TO SOMETHING AS TRAGIC AS A FUNERAL. I'VE NEVER THOUGHT LITTLE CHILDREN SHOULD BE TOLD ABOUT DEATH.

LET THEM KEEP THEIR INNOCENCE AS LONG AS THEY CAN.

GLAD TO SEE THIS SETTLED.

SHE'LL REST IN PEACE NOW.

SHE'S WITH HER OWN.

DADDY SHOULD MAKE HELEN ONE OF THOSE.

I THINK SHE'D LIKE TO HAVE ONE, DON'T YOU?

IT WOULD LOOK VERY PRETTY.

More stories by Mary Downing Hahn

What We Saw
The Thirteenth Cat
The Puppet's Payback and Other Chilling Tales
Guest
The Girl in the Locked Room
One for Sorrow
Took
Where I Belong
Mister Death's Blue-Eyed Girls
The Doll in the Garden
Closed for the Season
The Ghost of Crutchfield Hall
Deep and Dark and Dangerous
Witch Catcher
The Old Willis Place
Hear the Wind Blow
Anna on the Farm
Promises to the Dead
Anna All Year Round
As Ever, Gordy
Following My Own Footsteps
The Gentleman Outlaw and Me
Look for Me by Moonlight
Time for Andrew
The Wind Blows Backward
Stepping on the Cracks
The Spanish Kidnapping Disaster
The Dead Man in Indian Creek
December Stillness
Following the Mystery Man
Tallahassee Higgins
Wait Till Helen Comes
The Jellyfish Season
Daphne's Book
The Time of the Witch
The Sara Summer

The Creative Team

Scott Peterson is the editor of Detective Comics, DC Comics' flagship title; writer of *Batman: Gotham Adventures*; and co-creator of not one, but two new Batgirl comics. He has written children's books, animation, webcomics, music reviews, and novels and is the author of the acclaimed original graphic novel *Truckus Maximus*. He lives in the Pacific Northwest with his wife, children's author Melissa Wiley, and their children.

Meredith Laxton is an illustrator, comic artist, and proud parent of two chubby cats. Prior to creating comics full-time, Meredith worked in the video game industry creating artwork and graphics for both indie and major studios. Their most notable published work includes titles such as *MPLS Sound*, *The Crow: Hark The Herald*, and *Charlie's Spot #1–4*. They are based in Savannah, Georgia.

Russ Badgett has been making comics for several years, recently shifting toward color as his primary focus of study and practice. Titles of previous note include *Bloody Hel* as well as cover colors for IDW's *Ghostbusters: Answer the Call*. He currently resides in the hilly part of Texas.

Morgan Martinez has worked in comics since 2011, lettering everything from *Teen Titans Go!* for DC Comics to acclaimed indies such as *Heathen*, *The Curie Society*, and John Leguizamo's *Freak*. When she isn't working on comics, Morgan's interests include writing, drawing, gaming, queer rights, trans liberation, and being as unserious as circumstances allow. She lives in the South Bronx with her wife and their cat, Darcy.

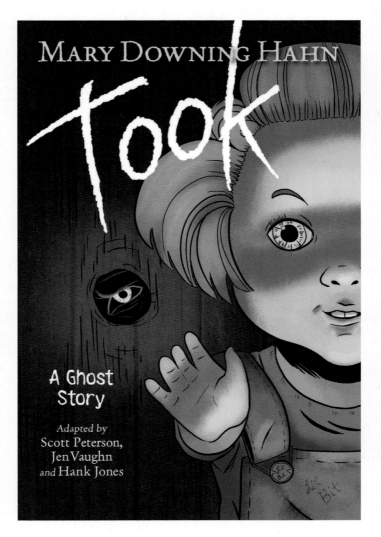